AF508187

the Attentionist

new choices for a new world

mitra manesh

Published by ISTS, 2026

ISBN:
979-8-9933904-0-6, paperback
979-8-9933904-1-3, ebook

www.mitramanesh.com
books@mitramanesh.com

CONTENTS

Dear Reader,

If this book is in your hands, something in you is already listening. Maybe to a question. Maybe to a quiet knowing. Maybe to a longing you haven't yet named.

I come from a long line of storytellers and teachers. So when I finally sat down to share the lessons life has offered me, it felt only natural they would arrive wrapped in story. The fiction in this book serves as a gentle scaffold for truths we are all living—truths that speak to our time with both urgency and invitation.

Over the years, I've had the privilege of working with thousands of people—from boardrooms to classrooms to bedrooms—across cultures and continents. And wherever I've gone, I've encountered a familiar ache: a quiet, persistent suffering shaped by survival and fear. It lives in our nervous systems, colors our relationships, and whispers that we are broken, separate, and alone.

The Attentionist was born in response to that whisper. Attentionism is the antidote to Survivalism. It's about awakening choice, expanding perspective, and consciously choosing what most benefits ourselves and the world. Attention is usually thought of in terms of efficiency and focus, but I see it as a gateway to transformation, a way to reimagine how we live, love, and lead.

This book weaves stories, tools, and lived truths that I have taught and trusted in real life. I hope that you live the book as well. That you let it slow you down and bring you back to what matters most. May it remind you that your attention is a sacred force, and that how—and where—you place it is an act of creation. And that you are not alone on this path.

With an open heart,
Mitra

ACKNOWLEDGMENTS

To my life partner, Henry—thank you for walking beside me, and for lifting me when I could no longer walk on my own. Your clarity of mind, your writer's craft, and your unwavering heart carried this book—our shared child—across its finish line.

To my firstborn, Melody—you sat with me in stillness, asked with curiosity, and transcribed my truths before I even knew they belonged on the page. You didn't just help me begin—you reminded me where the beginning was.

To my youngest, Tiffany— your work lives in the world of purely artistic books, yet you stepped into this with dearness and love. With your precision, designer's eye, and deep care, you helped me see its soul more clearly, and gave it form and beauty to match.

To my students, across decades and continents, your questions, doubts, and presence gave this work its practicality and pulse.

To my teachers—Grandma Ozra, Mom and Dad, Minoo and Mehran, Mr. Pourjahani, Dr. Vivekananda, and Francis Rothluebber. To Rumi—whose journey and words have guided me across lifetimes and silences, beyond time and form. To the many seen and unseen guides who showed me how to seek and speak the truth, and to those who taught me by contrast, through what not to do or be—I thank you.

YEKI-BOOD,

YEKI-NABOOD

In the fascinating mid-21st century, when the world was changing with unparalleled consequence and speed, there lived a technological wizard named Milan.

Milan was deeply concerned about the destruction, and self-destruction, of life on Earth.

He had broken many norms and codes, inventing life-enhancing technologies in fields like medicine, transportation, communications, artificial intelligence, climate change, and more. But it wasn't enough.

Earthlings lived by the creed of every man for himself, and the planet was spinning out of control: war was everywhere, nature in convulsions, species dying left and right. In a desperate effort to save the day, Milan masterminded a singular plan. He had discovered a distant planet, named it Ours, and figured out how to make it habitable for humans in the hope of creating a new start, a new chance, and a new life. Were there other living beings on the new planet? Perhaps. At this point, Milan didn't care. That would be a problem for the future. Besides, he was only really concerned about the survival of the species to which he belonged.

Atmospheric design, portable gravity, water crystallization, intergalactic rocket science—Milan had hired experts in a host of fantastical fields to address the unprecedented challenges of his radical plan. But something was missing. He knew no matter how great and technologically advanced life on planet Ours might be, suffering and destruction would follow the human race if those moving there did not learn and grow from their experiences.

A new kind of intelligence, of wisdom, was necessary. Milan wasn't exactly sure what sort of teacher or knowledge he was looking for, but he had to find someone who could identify what Earthlings needed to learn and change in order to avoid bringing the same mess to Ours that they had created over millennia on Earth.

To that end, Milan tasked his global team of sophisticated head-hunters to find the greatest teacher alive, someone who could diagnose the issues that brought Earth to its present state, and prescribe realistic remedies for turning things around. This expensive and expansive search took his team over many moons to many rooms across the globe, to no avail.

in search of the teacher

Milan and his team met and talked to numerous teachers, virtually and in person, from East to West, and many places in between. There were so many teachers to interview.

- Teachers well-known locally and globally.
- Teachers who lived in luxury and frequented celebrity homes and events, and those who lived a humble life and rejected opulence.
- Teachers who created institutions, communities, and even cults.
- Teachers with millions of followers and successful brands.
- Teachers with revolutionary vocabulary who operated underground.
- Teachers who grounded their wisdom in science and evidence and appealed to academic institutions and individuals.
- Teachers who mastered the popular trends and 'isms with charm and traveled the roads of fashionable spirituality to great success.

But none of these teachers were able to satisfy Milan's hunger for the deep knowing worthy of the world he wanted to create far away in space. Milan was looking for a different kind of insight that could unfold the mystery of self-destruction and suffering on Earth and offer new understanding and tools for an elevated life on planet Ours. He had no name or qualification for this teacher, but knew he needed to find him, or her, or them, and fast.

a teacher is found

Disappointed with his team's unsuccessful search, Milan was losing hope in this critical endeavor, and his excitement gradually gave way to concern and distress. One day, he sat dejected in his favorite chair looking at a 180-degree view of the ocean from his living room, when his teenage daughter, Kuriozi, came home from school. When she saw the state he was in, she asked, "What's wrong, Dad? Why are you so sad?"

Milan gave her a startled look—"That's what I usually ask you," he replied, then added softly: "I'm sad because my research team, with all of their expertise, education, and resources, has failed to find the right teacher, the wisest person on Earth!"

Kuriozi's face lit up with sudden excitement: "That's why you're sad? I can solve your problem. I know the best teacher and the wisest person on Earth. Just give me the job and I'll take you to meet her!"

Milan burst out laughing. Then, half curious and half serious, he said, "You got it Kuriozi, you got the job. Take me to her and you'll be handsomely compensated, just like my research team."

The lighthearted exchange lifted the mood in the room. For Kuriozi, it was a rare moment of feeling good in relation to her dad;

he had taken her seriously despite her age, and she felt important, seen. She offered her hand to seal the deal. Father and daughter walked together to the kitchen, where Milan poured Kuriozi a glass of *chicha*—a festive ancestral Amazonian drink he'd brought back from a recent trip to Ecuador.

It's not easy being a teenager, Kuriozi thought as she looked up at Milan, who suddenly felt close, like an equal, a friend. *Especially when your dad is super smart, desperately trying to save the world, and clueless about what's going on in his own family, especially me.*

they have a date

The next day came and went with no mention of the previous day's agreement. Milan assumed Kuriozi had forgotten all about it until he received a text from her in the middle of the day with a few suggested times for meeting. Impressed with his daughter's focus and follow-through, he agreed to one of the proposed times. He felt excited—maybe even elated—at the thought of meeting the person Kuriozi considered to be wise.

The day finally arrived, and Milan did his best to keep his expectations in check. After all, he was one of the most advanced thinkers of his time, looking for the most extraordinary teacher of his time, so he knew the bar was impossibly high for someone his teenage daughter might know and recommend. *And yet…* Milan couldn't help but wonder. He decided to go in with an open mind, ask for no details before the meeting, and bring Kuriozi along.

They drove in Milan's latest invention—a sleek, air-powered sports coupe that was turning heads everywhere. Kuriozi had hoped and yearned for some alone time and loving connection with her dad, as he was usually too distant or preoccupied to be with her that way. But as soon as he got in the car, Milan called his office, and when that was done he immediately thought-selected some music from a telepathic sound system he had recently patented. All of which made the connection Kuriozi longed for impossible. Disappointed and unsettled, she settled for being driven by her dad with no one else in the car!

The address was only 15 minutes from home but felt like a world apart. As Milan slowly drove through the open gate of the property, he noted the variety of trees, vegetable gardens, butterflies, streams, and other natural life that adorned Matria's land. He couldn't help comparing this setting to his own manicured greeneries, meticulously designed by famed landscape architects; the contrast was strangely humbling, the rigorous human pursuit of perfection in his garden at home vs. the imperfect but stunning design of nature.

Milan parked his car and walked with Kuriozi to the front of the property. He found the door to the house open, just like the gate had been. He felt almost nervous, as if on a blind date, but he settled immediately when he saw a gentle and warm woman come towards him. Matria greeted Kuriozi first with a long, loving hug.

Then Kuriozi introduced her dad. "This is my dad Milan, the smartest and busiest person on Earth, or so they say! And *this* is Matria, the wisest and kindest teacher on Earth, so I say!"

With Kuriozi's introduction, the ice was broken, and both Matria and Milan chuckled as they greeted one another, and stepped inside.

where do we start?

Milan settled comfortably into a cushioned seat next to Kuriozi, who felt wonderful playing matchmaker between her father and her favorite person in life. For reasons she couldn't fully explain, her excitement and happiness brought tears to her eyes. Perhaps it was the fleeting sense of family, alive and present for her with both Matria and her dad by her side, something she hadn't felt in a long time.

Milan broke the silence first. "Do you know why I'm here, Matria?"

Matria offered a playful smile. "I can guess, but I have a feeling you'd like to tell me yourself."

Milan returned her smile. "Indeed I would. But before I forget, I need to ask you about your garden and the butterflies I saw on my way in. I can't believe you have any! They're so rare these days. I read just this morning how dangerously close to extinction they are."

"Yes," Matria replied, "and what a tragic loss for the planet that would be—physically, energetically, symbolically. Butterflies hold the lightness of life, the secret of transformation. They show us the journey from crawling to flying, and we need that now more than ever. But I *know* they will survive and thrive—if not here, then elsewhere. As for my garden," Matria lowered her voice with the cheeky confidentiality of a cook giving away a special recipe, "I've never used anything toxic on this land, and that of course helps."

Milan sighed and shook his head. "I wish I shared your confidence. Butterflies are exactly why I'm here. We've damaged this planet, and everything in it, beyond repair. That's why I plan to colonize a new world, planet Ours. My aim is to take the most knowledgeable experts with me to build a life that's both sustainable and far more advanced than what we've created here on Earth. I've gathered the most brilliant minds to make planet

Ours truly *ours*. What I'm missing…" Milan paused, not quite sure how to finish.

Before he could, Matria jumped in, with a wink to Kuriozi, "…is loving hearts to consort with those brilliant minds and create the harmonious, joyful melodies of life."

Kuriozi beamed. Milan nodded, cautiously. "Well, that's a *poetic* way of putting it. But do you think you can help us achieve what we want to achieve? And if so, where should we start this conversation?"

"That all depends on where you want to go, and why you want to go there. Beginnings are always informed by the destination, and vice versa."

"Yes, of course," Milan quickly agreed, not entirely sure of what he was agreeing to. Then, confidently: "I'm interested in learning all about the wisdom of survival."

Matria reached out and touched Milan gently on the arm. "Wisdom, my dear, is not something you learn. It's something you remember, and once we remember our wisdom, we can let go of survival, and aim for *thrival*."

AQ

Milan wasn't sure what to make of Matria's answer, so he shifted his approach. "Who do *you* consider to be wise?"

"Everybody," Matria replied without hesitation. "In their essence, that is. But most people are out of touch with their essence. That's why a wise person is someone with a high AQ."

"AQ?" Milan repeated, puzzled. "You mean *IQ*?"

"No," Matria said, "I mean AQ."

"I've never heard of AQ before."

"Most people haven't, although that will soon change." A teasing glint appeared in Matria's eyes. "Of all people, Milan, you who are planning to take humanity from one planet to another shouldn't be looking for old terminologies or what you already know."

Milan colored slightly. He glanced at Kuriozi, who was following the conversation wide-eyed. Collecting himself, he summoned a smile. "Fair point, Matria. I am all about innovation. So tell me more about yours."

"This isn't about innovation," Matria corrected again. "It's about creation."

A puzzled expression spread across Milan's face. "Between AQ and creation, I think you've lost me. Maybe I'm not as sharp in the wisdom business as I am in other kinds of business."

Matria laughed out loud, a bit too loud for Milan's comfort. "Vocabulary is telling," she said. "Wisdom is *not* a business, though many have turned it into one. But I'm glad your curiosity is awakened, Milan. That's the first step. Let's walk gently and slowly together down the roads of unfolding deeper knowing."

Unfamiliar with her vocabulary and unsure where this conversation was heading, Milan was relieved to let Matria lead the way.

yes, attention quotient

Matria began: "AQ reflects one's ability to pay intentional attention, followed by wise action, rather than sleepwalking through life on autopilot. The 'A' stands for Attention, and the 'Q' for Quotient.

"People with a high degree of AQ are grounded in the present, aware of the choices available to them, and capable of choosing what serves them best. They go beyond a programmed life designed by others. They choose the experiences and life *they* want to examine and explore. They create.

"Creation is our birthright. When we wake up to our choices and abilities, we start creating, I mean truly creating, not for profit or to impress others, but for the natural joy of creation itself. All human beings are creators, but most of the time most of us create in a Survivalist state of fear, chasing some form of advantage: wealth, fame or acceptance by the crowd. We do this because we don't know our true origin, the extent of our powers, and the nature of our relationship with one another and the Source.

"So, to rekindle our true power of creation, we need to first unfold our Story—who we are and where we come from. That can help us understand ourselves better, raise our AQ, and create in new ways. Which is what you're looking for, right Milan?"

"Yes…" Milan said, a little uneasily. Matria's speech was full of new ideas, and he hadn't really come to hear a "Story." After a bit of silence, he stated: "I don't quite understand what you mean yet, but I'm open to how and where you would like to start."

As he said these words, Milan was surprised at his own flexibility. He normally had little patience for fanciful tales and odd digressions. But on this day and in the presence of Matria—and Kuriozi—he found himself receptive and even-tempered. At least for now.

the creation story

As Milan settled in, ready to hear the Story, Matria quietly got up and left the room. A few minutes later she returned carrying a tray of herbal teas, an assortment of fruits, and a small bowl of unshelled nuts.

Smiling deeply, she said: "Everything on this tray is from the land you drove by to get here. From the spearmint in our tea to the fruits and nuts on our plates. This abundant, generous land feeds me and all my guests. Isn't that superb?"

Milan mumbled something, half grumble, half sigh, which led to a cheeky eye exchange between Kuriozi and Matria. She finished pouring the tea, made herself comfortable in her seat, and began:

"'*Yeki-bood, yeki-nabood.*'" So begins every story from ancient Persia. *Yeki-bood* means the visible world. *Yeki-nabood*, the invisible. These are the two realms in which we live; matter and energy, the duality of life on Earth.

"Once, long ago, in a realm outside of time and space, there existed only Everything, still, complete, and undivided. It's unknown why or how, but somehow a movement began, and Everything grew curious about unfolding Itself. That curiosity eventually led Everything to create aspects of Itself. Among the many aspects that were created were boundless Little-Everythings to help the one Big-Everything explore and expand, and many Darlings to witness the marvel of this exploration and expansion, like spectators at a light and magic show that astonished without end. Darlings did not participate in the show, but they loved watching and they had a very important role to play, which I'll tell you more about later on.

"Because Little-Everythings were new to existence, big-Everything provided them with a blueprint to guide them and show them how to create. Not a rigid blueprint, but an ever-expanding, responsive blueprint based on love and unity. The purpose of this blueprint was to safeguard connection, encourage creation, and facilitate the collective expansion of Little-Everythings."

same map, different roads

Matria went quiet and took a few more sips of her tea.

Kuriozi, who was listening intently, asked: "What is a blueprint? I mean, *I know,* but...?"

"It's a map," Milan said, without taking his eyes off Matria. He was eager—impatient is more like it—to hear more of the Story and figure out whether Matria could help him or not.

Matria turned to Kuriozi: "That's right, dear, a map. All of these Little-Everythings happily and uniquely created many marvelous things using the same map while having fun and playful experiences. They created tiny little wonders like bubbles and halos and infinite shades of blue, as well as large, impressive universes, multiverses, and megaverses. They shared their diverse creations generously and willingly. There was great delight in the way the Little-Everythings created so uniquely on their own and shared so entirely with each other."

"But how could they create different things while following the same map?" Kuriozi asked.

"An excellent question, Kuriozi. The same way that art students can go to the same school, listen to the same lectures, and read the same books but create different kinds of art. The blueprint, or map, as Milan called it, only showed them the landmarks they needed to consider; it never dictated what they needed to create. They were free to create as they wished, as long as they had unity, love, and expansion in their heart, and created under the same light."

the fall-of-consciousness?

Despite himself, Milan was intrigued by Matria's words. But suddenly, a counter impulse flared, and he pulled himself up short. "Where are we going with this Story, anyway?"

"We're not going anywhere, dear. In fact, we're returning home with this Story."

Milan looked at Kuriozi's face, which was full of excitement and anticipation, and decided to follow her lead.

Matria continued: "And that is what creation looked like, Big-Everything simply creating many Little-Everythings who could create, share and grow in joy, *until…*"

Kuriozi couldn't help herself—"Until *what*, Matria?"

"Until the Fall-of-Consciousness."

For a moment the three sat in silence. Milan felt like *he* was falling, or at least drifting far from his usual orbit of ideas. "Did you say the Fall-of-Consciousness?" he asked.

Matria nodded, undeterred. "I did. You see, at our core we all have the same origin, are interconnected, and made from the same love energy. But there came a time when some of the Little-Everythings started to leave all that behind."

"Why would they leave these good things behind?" Kuriozi asked.

"Well, they didn't do it knowingly," Matria explained. "An anomaly occurred when a Little-Everything, unintentionally and accidently, started creating without following the blueprint for connection, creativity, and growth. This turned that Little-Everything into a Something! You could say this was the birth of the first Something."

who is "something"?

"OK, we've gone from Everything to Something," Milan said, with a hint of sarcasm that came from many years of being in charge, and hailed by all as the smartest guy in the room. He regretted it immediately when he looked at Kuriozi. "Not really sure what that means or where we're heading. Who, and what, are Somethings?"

"Let me try again, Milan. This is very important, as I'm sure you'll agree. A Something is a Little-Everything who has chosen to create apart from Big-Everything, and without consideration for others or following the blueprint."

"Was that bad?" Kuriozi pressed. "What happened to the first Something?"

"Well, once this Little-Everything became the first Something, it realized it could create faster and easier, and other Little-Everythings gradually noticed the Something's new ways, and they too got excited and curious about a new way of creating.

"Little-Everythings wondered what it was like to be different and separate, and create without sharing. You see, they were naive in their oneness. They couldn't imagine that being a Something could do any harm, because they had no concept of causing one another pain. They had never hurt, or been hurt; their only experience was playing, having fun, and sharing their creations with each other."

As Milan listened, part of him felt like he had as a young boy, when his grandmother read him ancient tales that ignited his imagination and moved his heart. But his rational mind had a different agenda. It was looking for something solid and scientific, and that interfered with his curiosity and enjoyment. At the same time, he felt something that he had not felt for a long time… a heart connection, perhaps? He felt affectionate toward both Kuriozi and Matria. He could understand his feeling for Kuriozi, but Matria?

Milan's musings were gently interrupted by Kuriozi's voice. "Did Little-Everythings continue to play with Something?" she asked.

"Indeed they did," Matria replied. "In fact, they really liked the way Something was playing, so much so that they told Big-Everything all about Something's new discovery. They shared their enthusiasm about this new mode of creation and playing, and asked Big-Everything if they too could play and create like Something.

"Big-Everything, who saw Little-Everythings' eagerness and curiosity, gave their blessing for them to create and play without the blueprint, if they so desired. This marked the birth of choice. Now Little-Everythings had the choice of creating under Big-Everything's light, based on the blueprint, or under their own light, without the blueprint, like Something. Little-Everythings loved having this choice. And so, many of the trusting Little-Everythings followed Something's lead."

the power to choose
and the power to create

The birth of choice, Milan thought to himself. Now that's an interesting turn. "How did having a choice change Little-Everythings," he heard himself ask?

A lengthy silence followed as Matria slowly peeled a large orange and distributed it to her guests. Milan smacked his lips. "Delicious," he said, and turned to Matria with a smile. It was his first true smile of the visit. "*Well?*" he asked, as if there had been no break in the conversation.

Matria continued: "*Well*, this new and exciting experience eventually led many Little-Everythings to choose to become Somethings. They chose to create on their own. You see, Little-Everythings now had both the power to create and the power to choose, a rarity in the realm of beings."

"How extraordinary," Milan observed. "It never occurred to me that choice and creativity might be rare and special gifts, especially when paired. We take them for granted."

Kuriozi was hanging on every word. "Then what happened?" she asked.

The corners of Matria's eyes crinkled with delight. "Then those Somethings gave birth to other Somethings. Well, not exactly. When Somethings gave birth to new beings, they always began as Little-Everythings. However, slowly they were shaped into Somethings by those around them. Knowingly or unknowingly, they were taught about separation and consequent wanting, which evolved through eons into wanting more and more, until, eventually, they wanted it all, and then wanted it all for themselves.

"The fast and easy way of creating without consideration for anyone else gradually diminished Somethings' connection with each other, as well as their memory of the choice they had to live under the light again. They lost their unity and their sense of play and joy. This brought about many new conditions like fear, comparison, anger, jealousy, greed, domination, competition, and other kinds of suffering. All of which spread like a virus amongst the Somethings. Things became heavier, dramas were formed, and traumas experienced. And this, my dears, was the Fall-of-Consciousness. Let me be more precise—there was no real fall, just the density of fear taking over the lightness of love."

everything's role

Matria's words shifted the tone in the room. Something somber had arrived. Milan thought of the butterflies and the special light-ness Matria said they had. "Why didn't Big-Everything stop the Fall-of-Consciousness?" he asked.

"In order to do that, Big-Everything would have to compromise the choice it had given Little-Everythings, and make decisions for them," Matria said. "Even though Big-Everything was fully aware of what was going on, it honored the gift it had offered Little-Everythings. It was up to Somethings to choose and become Little-Everythings again. It was sad that the light of unity became a forgotten choice, but it was what it was.

"Big-Everything did however take measures to protect other beings from the potential contamination of the viruses created by Somethings. As the contamination raged, Big-Everything called all Somethings and asked them to make another choice—either go back to being Little-Everythings, or leave and go their separate way so they wouldn't affect other beings in the Land-of-Unity. Some stayed as Little-Everythings, and many left as Somethings. Those who left became even more separated from Big-Everything, as well as Little-Everythings, Darlings, and eventually each other and even themselves!"

"I forgot about your Darlings," Milan exclaimed. "You men-tioned them earlier. What are they all about? What's their role?"

Matria laughed. "I wondered when one of you might ask. I've made up the name Darlings to refer to many different beings. They're all non-physical, with different abilities and roles, but one thing in common—they know the things that Somethings have forgotten. After the Fall-of-Consciousness, Darlings witnessed the suffering of Somethings and asked Big-Everything if they could stop being mere spectators and actively help Somethings remember who they really were. Permission was granted with one condition—they could only assist if and when Somethings made the choice to go from being Somethings to becoming Little-Everythings again. Basically, Darlings could not initiate Something's journey of recollection, but they could facilitate it."

"Are Darlings like angels," Kuriozi inquired?

Matria laughed again, reached for Kuriozi's hand, and said: "Dear one, angels mean different things to different people. Do you remember having imaginary friends as a kid?"

"I do. Those were often the only friends I had!"

Milan's heart dropped as he remembered that he too had deep relationships with imaginary friends as a child, especially after classmates started labeling him odd. He had no idea his daughter also suffered from isolation and rejection. His eyes welled up with tenderness that he hadn't felt in a long time.

Matria continued gently: "Well, Darlings are adults' invisible friends who truly exist, except without body and form. Some exist to help Somethings remember to create like Little-Everythings again; some are teachers with deep experience and understanding to guide this journey; and all are waiting to share what they know and walk beside us as we rediscover what we have lost. They miss watching all the Little-Everythings play!"

As Matria spoke, a cat with fluffy white hair and mysterious green eyes entered the room, stopped before Milan, and hopped into his lap. Milan stiffened, but when the cat started to purr, he smiled and relaxed.

"*Now there's a* Darling*!*" Matria exclaimed. "I mean, literally, her name is *Darling.* And she probably came in just now because she heard us use the word. On the other hand, she might really be a Darling. Either way, it's always a good sign when beings far more energetic than us find us attractive and safe and wish to express their warmth and love in our lap."

"Didn't you say Darlings are invisible and non-physical?" Kuriozi asked, staring with wonder at her dad and the cat.

"Yes, they are purely energetic, but they can communicate through anything—birds, cats, clouds, dreams, a gentle breeze. Butterflies seem to be an especially favorite host, at least in my world. That said, they frequently work on their own, unseen, with magical energies that can change our state of mind and life from one day to the next. They are a tremendous force, just waiting for an invitation to help us remember 'everything' we have forgotten."

Milan was smiling deeply and stroking the *Darling* in his lap. It was now Kuriozi's turn to feel tears in her eyes.

"Why can't Darlings, who know so much and are such good friends to Somethings, just make the rise of consciousness happen?" she asked.

"Remember, Darlings are non-physical," Matria explained. "The Fall-of-Consciousness took place in the physical world, because of the choices Little-Everythings made, so it can only rise again in the physical world, through the choices Little-Everythings—who are now Somethings—make. Darlings can help, but the job of a good friend is never to do our journey for us. Rather, it's to walk alongside us on our journey, and share what they know—if and only if we want to know."

systems and institutions

Kuriozi was lost in thought, and memory. The conversation about Darlings had triggered something in her. A strange smile played upon her lips. Suddenly, she noticed Milan looking at her, and quickly turned to Matria.

"So what became of Somethings in the new land?"

Matria continued with her story. "Well, first and foremost, the separation affected Somethings' identity. As their original lightness turned more dense, their ability to create uniquely dimmed, and more and more they just copied one another.

"Because the delight of creating individually and expanding collectively was gone, Somethings stopped caring about what they made, and began caring about how they could win and impress other Somethings in order to feel good. The lack of originality and tendency to copy spread among the Somethings until it became the collective norm.

"Eventually, this led to the creation of systems and institutions, and a belief that acceptance by these institutions and their members was more important than creation itself. Fitting in, copying, mimicking, and being just like each other became the most important thing to most Somethings. Subconsciously, they still wanted to be together, but now, instead of enjoying the true unity of Little-Everythings, they enjoyed sameness. They all strived to be part of the same class, club, tribe, religion, region, or any other informal or formal system or institution that they thought mattered the most."

Kuriozi shuddered: "I wouldn't want to be just like everybody else. But I don't understand; what was the main job of these systems and institutions?"

"Believe it or not, their main job was to *un-teach* connection, creativity, and true love in young Little-Everythings, and ensure their allegiance and obedience as Somethings. In fear, the keepers of these systems and institutions created conflicts of all kinds, including wars and atrocities in order to take or hold power over others."

Kuriozi was still perplexed "Why didn't Somethings get rid of systems and keepers that turned out so bad?"

Matria let out an uncharacteristically weary breath. "Easier said than done. The systems and institutions that older Somethings created were so clever and effective that newer Somethings forgot how and why they created them. They insisted that they always were and always would be, and pretended it was the natural way. They were so successful at this that Somethings often turned to these very institutions when they were lost, believing their captors were the ones to set them free.

"Sometimes, when younger and free-minded Somethings objected, the institutions pretended to change, like chameleons, just enough to convince Somethings they were free. They used the right language with the wrong intentions and actions, and they cast an amnesia over their own machinations and roles. Above all, they kept Somethings in a fearful mode of survival, believing they always needed protection, that they were always unsafe and unsure."

who are the survivalists?

As if in protest, the sound of birds chirping loudly in Matria's garden suddenly filled the room, then settled and disappeared. After a few moments, Milan picked up the thread. "This is a fascinating mythological tale Matria, but how does it relate to my plan to take the best of the best to planet Ours?"

Matria looked at Milan with good-humored candor. "I see as much as I gained your attention, I failed to clarify the essence of the story as it relates to us. You see, the Somethings in this story are us, and the land of physicality that we moved to is Earth. *We* have become the Survivalists I've been describing, regardless of what we own and what we know."

Milan fell into a deep silence, as if he was examining Matria's story from start to finish, searching for any mistakes or inaccuracies in his sharp mind. After a long pause, he said, "But a lot of what you mentioned in this story is not true in my case and in the case of many people I know or know of. We are creators; we know we have choices. We do not go along with systems. We are not who our parents and institutions wanted us to be!"

"True," Matria conceded. "Every now and then some light enters between the cracks, and some of us remember that we're creators with choice and powers beyond what they have untaught us. That's how we give birth to unique ideas, art, words, projects, findings, theories. But then most of us take our creations into the same old world of Somethingness and Survivalism and buy back into the lack of choice, or live in angry reaction to the old choices, or create new institutions that undermine choice even more."

Milan let out a low whistle. "This is a really dark claim, Matria. So in your view, are there any other states for us beside Survivalism, as you call it, on planet Earth? How do we find our way out of Something*ness,* into Something *else?*

Matria laughed: "That is indeed, the question. And we can find this 'Something *else*' in whatever we know to be true. Truth is always at hand, and always leads us to a better place. On Earth, there are three main states of being that describe the range between Somethings and Little-Everything, and that explain how close or far we are from union at any given time."

survivalist... attentionist... eternalist

Milan's shoulders sank, as if from overload. Then he smiled. "Okay, I'm taking the bait, tell me about the three states!"

Matria smiled back. She admired Milan's unusual blend of exasperation and curiosity. "I'm so glad you asked," she said. "The states are Survivalist, Attentionist, and Eternalist. These states have ranges within themselves, too, and are not black and white. Are you ready?"

Milan and Kuriozi nodded.

"By the way, this is no longer Story. This is an accurate account of how we live on Earth today. The Survivalist is mostly disconnected from self and source, in fear of the future or lamenting the past, and escaping from fabricated harms produced mainly by his-her-their own overly-activated, narrowly rational mind. Not all harms are illusory, of course. Sometimes there is real harm created by frightened Survivalists. But there is also a huge body of self-imposed harm and fear in this state. Survivalists live in prisons that they themselves construct, and can, and often do, turn something pleasant into its opposite, causing suffering to self and others. They have practiced Something-*ness* well, and lead their lives based on answering—and hence living—the following questions:

1. What is wrong—with me, the world, or the people in it?

2. Am I safe in this frightening and frightened world?
3. Do I fit in and am I accepted by—my family, community, school, faith group, workplace, or any number of systems, institutions, or tribes?"

Matria paused briefly and looked from Milan to Kuriozi and back to Milan again, as if to say, 'Are you with me so far?' She then continued. "The Attentionist is able to observe present-time experiences neutrally, use the past for growth and learning (as well as the healthy pleasures of memory), and plan the future, knowing that when it arrives it will be another present that can hold more and different options. Attentionists thrive in change because they know they are choice-makers, and hence they love expanding their choice-consciousness. They are Somethings en route to remembering their Little-Everything-*ness*, and they lead their lives based on answering—and hence living—the following questions:

1. What am I truly seeing or experiencing right now?
2. What are my other choices beyond what my frightened mind is offering me?
3. With well-being as my goal, what choice would serve me best in this moment?"

Matria paused again before endeavoring to share her thoughts about the highest state, Eternalism. When she spoke, her tone was quiet, but her eyes gently burned.

"Eternalists are mostly absorbed in union. They are here with physicality, but they know they are made of light and love and are not from here really. They pay more attention to their light than their density, and energy more than physicality. Eternalists are aware of their unlimited-ness, and enjoy their limited time here on Earth. Eternalists are awakened Somethings who are now Little-Everythings in physical form. They lead their lives based on answering—and hence living—the following questions:

1. How can I joyfully create, grow, and serve myself?
2. How can I serve and share what I create with others?
3. How can I become more like Big-Everything?"

Matria picked up her cup of tea, and drank what was left. Once again, the energy in the room had changed. "Most of us living on Earth are stuck in the Survivalist state," she continued. "However, that's changing rapidly, based on the choices made by some who have remembered their possibilities and decided as Attentionists—with the help of Darlings"—here Matria winked at Kuriozi—"to lighten the game of dense physicality.

"We're all being invited, gently or forcibly, depending on our degree of density, to face our choice-points during this unprece-dented time of change. Faster and vaster changes will continue to accelerate dangerously until we knowingly and intentionally decide who we are and where/how we want to live. Are we citizens of the Land-of-Unity, or the Land-of-Separation? Facades and pretenses will no longer hide our true home. It is our allegiance to the truth that matters, not our location, image, or brand."

physics and metaphysics

Survivalists, Attentionists, Eternalists. Milan felt his plans wobble and his feelings sink as he listened to Matria's words. If she was right, the challenge before him was far greater than he had imagined. With a frustrated and unfiltered tone, he said, "Quite a bomb to drop on me, Matria. I'm on a deadline here. I was hoping to get a few damn recommendations and bits of advice from you. Instead, I'm told we're all doomed Survivalists, apparently including myself, with only a few illusory moments of creative exception. Unless we can somehow change ourselves before it's too late and become the Attentionists or Eternalists you're talking about, which seems like a long-shot, forgive my being blunt. Of course, I may be underplaying the influence of Darlings," Milan added, with frustrated sarcasm, "so there's always that." Then, catching himself, he looked down at the *Darling* in his lap, who shifted position and purred more loudly than before.

Matria was unfazed by Milan's words and tone. "Do you notice your Survivalist language, emotions, and conclusions, Milan? You have seen the light through the cracks many times. You have remembered and taken action as a creator of new ideas, inventions, and even new ways of living and working. Nevertheless, a vision of a better future is a bomb dropped on you. A time frame is a deadline that you fear. The pleasant experience of hearing the truth destroys your hope and upsets you. If we don't see and accept where we are, we can never get to where we want to be. Just like the navigation systems your technologists so intelligently designed—they can only guide us to where we want to go if they first determine where we are. Do you see my point?"

Milan nodded, but his impatience was not so easily allayed. "I do, but I'm a realist. I'm interested in physics and technology, and you're speaking about metaphysics and mythology. Plus, we as a species don't have much time."

When he finished speaking, Matria smoothly rose to her feet and left the room. Milan was sure he had offended her. He looked at Kuriozi, who had been quiet for a while, and realized that she did not share his concern. She was smiling, glowing actually, not unlike Matria, so once again Milan decided to follow her lead and just wait.

Matria walked back with a piece of paper in her hand. She offered the paper to Milan with a smile that eliminated his fear of having given offense. "Here you are, dear Milan. Physics will soon catch up with metaphysics. That journey has already begun. Ask your neuroscientists. Please feel free to contact anyone on this list. These are Survivalists who have journeyed to the state of Attentionism and have their eyes on becoming Eternalists. Perhaps their stories will help you realize how mythology and life can help resolve Survivalist sufferings in a *real* way. Now, even though it has been an absolute treat to meet you, I would like to retreat to my own space."

With that, Matria gently kissed both Kuriozi's and Milan's heads, and with her hand on her heart, gracefully departed.

milan & kuriozi go home

Milan rose spontaneously out of respect as Matria left the room. He wasn't sure he could embrace her teachings, but he knew he had been in the presence of a deep and thoughtful soul. He walked toward Kuriozi and asked, "How did you say you know Matria?"

"I didn't, because you never asked," she answered, smiling playfully, but with an undertone of pain in her voice.

Milan saw the smile and missed—or decided to overlook—the rest. "Oh, that must have been before I learned to be curious like you. Allow me to ask now, how did you meet Matria, Madame Kuriozi?"

"Matria teaches us Attentionism at school. You should know that; after all, you are the one who created our school."

Milan laughed. "I might have created the school, but I don't run it. I'm really glad they hired Matria to teach the kids to pay attention better."

Before this day, Milan had never heard about "Attentionism," and he wasn't quite ready to ask Kuriozi anything about it. He had revealed too much weakness in one day in his daughter's presence.

Kuriozi shrugged her shoulders. "Maybe you should hire her to teach the adults too. It helps them remember they have choices at all times, and shows them how to work with their emotions and thoughts."

Milan wasn't sure how to take Kuriozi's suggestion, but he decided to end this conversation with a simple "thank you."

"Thank *you*, Dad. I'm so happy that you found Matria and her teachings. She has made a world of difference in my life and the life of my classmates."

When they got to their car, Milan was slower than normal and looked contemplative. Kuriozi was hugely stimulated and elated by the meeting, and smiled inwardly. But her feelings were complex, and bittersweet. They both chose silence for the ride back home, which, strangely, made them feel close. When they arrived, Milan felt different, with no words to explain the change except for this: he hugged Kuriozi—a very long and unusual hug—and told her he loved her.

Kuriozi was surprised by the hug. *That Darling, or cat, or whatever it was, must have gotten through to my dad,* she thought. *He's not usually emotionally expressive, certainly not like this. Caring, yes, but sharing, no.*

It was late, and father and daughter both had a lot to ponder. Not much was said, but a lot was felt and exchanged as they ended this unusual day by heading toward their respective bedrooms.

new observations

The next morning Milan got up earlier than usual and sent a message to the first person on the list Matria had given him: Sukseso. Surprisingly, Sukseso answered immediately even though it was 5:30 am and they were in the same time zone. It didn't take long before they agreed on a time and a place to meet. Milan was impressed with Sukseso's efficiency and clarity.

He found himself thinking about Matria's words as he went about his day, replaying what she'd told him over and over in his head. He wondered about Little-Everythings, Somethings, Darlings, Survivalists, Attentionists, and Eternalists. New words, new concepts, new stories.

Even though Milan was a man of science and instinctively resisted much of what Matria had to say, her core ideas, if not her Story, resonated with him, and this was validated by his observations throughout the day. It was a busy one, with important meetings and important people—a head of a state, a genius inventor, and the CEO of the largest AI company in the world. Milan listened and paid close attention to them all, and lo and behold, Matria was right. One tried hard to prove how powerful he was, the next how intelligent, the third how visionary and ahead of his time. As successful and important as these luminaries were outwardly, he sensed that inside each there lived a frightened Survivalist, regardless of the position, knowledge, and the powers they held.

Milan continued paying attention to how people around him spoke, thought, and behaved, in personal and professional settings, in gatherings, in the media and on social platforms. The more he heard and observed, the more he realized how common Survivalism was. He also started to observe his own language and thought patterns, and was often startled by what he found.

Milan's team noticed how he had become more attentive and present. They started to whisper and wonder if this was a sign of a new project or invention. No one suspected what was about to unfold.

SUKSESO

A PHYSICAL ATTENTIONIST

Milan didn't pay much attention to Sukseso's last name or address, but when he arrived at their residence, he realized he was meeting one of the most successful people in the business world. Sukseso had made a fortune in real estate, then made headlines by giving most of it away. Later, they designed a popular app that helped millions identify and track an innovative series of markers for inner wealth. It was the first cooperatively-owned app in the world. All users shared the profit based on the level of their own growth, their assistance to the growth of others, and/or contributing toward the enhancement of the app.

Sukseso greeted Milan warmly at their splendid and welcoming home. They looked fit and grounded, and felt humble and kind. Their roundish face was brimming with good cheer, and ornamented with a quiet smile. They led Milan toward a fruit and vegetable garden on the side of their large property and the two sat in the middle of greeneries, on a colorful Persian carpet placed on a wooden surface with many cushions all around. In the distance, the hum of a lively crowd that had gathered on Sukseso's farm next to their residence could be heard.

"I didn't realize you had company today," Milan said, with a nod towards the farm. "If I had known, I would've come another time."

"Oh, I have guests every day," Sukseso replied. "Hundreds, in fact. The land before you is rich with organic produce, and our gates are open to those who wish to pick, cook, and share their food in a communal setting, from 7 a.m. to 7 p.m., 7 days a week. Locals call it the *Grow and Glow* event."

"*Organic produce*," Milan exclaimed. "That's amazing. Experts say the earth can't produce organically anymore. I can't believe you're giving yours away. Aren't you afraid you'll run out and not have enough for yourself and your loved ones?"

Sukseso's smile blossomed into hearty laughter. "Experts have agendas, my friend. But if we treat the land well, the more you pick, the more it gives. Nature is abundant."

Milan smiled at the news of Sukeso's harvest, and the fact that they shared it with whoever passed by. *They must be well off indeed,* he thought, as he turned to his host: "I must say, I didn't expect to meet a famously wealthy person such as yourself when I called you up. After all, Matria is very un-worldly, at least in her ideas, don't you agree? How do you know her?"

"Oh, she's un-worldly, alright," Sukseso concurred, with a glint in their eyes, "but in the best of ways. I met her through my son. Matria teaches Attentionism at his school, and when I ended up in the hospital with a heart attack a few years ago, my son heard my doctor saying I need to pay better attention to the way I lead my life. He told me, 'I know the perfect person who can help you with that.' In my state of despair, I had no resistance and said yes to my son's invitation. And that's how I met Matria."

"How curious," Milan said. "I met her through my daughter. She seems to have an interesting relationship with the young. But before we go on, could you please tell me what Attentionism is? Both Matria and my daughter used this term the other day, and I'm not sure I know what it really means."

"Of course," Sukseso grinned. "Attentionism is a term made up by Matria. She likes to play with words and make up new ones to introduce new ways of understanding the terms of life. All words are made up by someone anyway, so why not her?"

"True, and those funny new words stick to your memory like glue," Milan followed, two-thirds compliment and one-third complaint. "I haven't been able to let go of Survivalist, Attentionist, and Eternalist since I met Matria, not to mention

AQ, Little-Everythings, Somethings, and Darlings!"

"Yes, she has a gift for that, and a purpose," Sukseso brightly rejoined. "New vocabulary, new consciousness, and a new world that she is passionate to help create. But let me share with you what I know about Attentionism."

Savoring the chance to impart what they knew to Milan, Sukseso began: "As Matria says, there are two worlds that we live in, *yeki-bood* and *yeki-nabood,* the visible and the invisible. As there are two worlds, so there are two currencies. In the visible world, the currency is money, whichever form you exchange it in. You want something, somehow you pay for it and that thing becomes yours. In the invisible world, the currency is *attention.* You believe something is of value, you *pay attention* to it, and that experience becomes yours.

"In essence, most of us most of the time are seeking one or another or both of these currencies; attention or money, which is fame or fortune, or attention *and* money, which is fame *and* fortune!"

Milan laughed. "That's true. I know lots of people who are fixated on one or the other, and sometimes both."

"Yeah, but here's the wrinkle—most of us care more about how we spend our money than we do about how we spend our attention. Even though attention is far more valuable than money. We have a variety of financial advisors and coaches, but we don't have attentional advisors or Attentionist coaches."

"Wait a second," Milan asked, "how is attention more valuable than money?"

"Think about it," Sukseso replied. "If attention was real estate, it would be the most expensive real estate on Earth. Are you aware of the cost of 30-second advertising on prime-time TV, or the cover of any popular magazine, or the feed of any well-known influencer? Business and marketing experts know all too well the value of our attention. That's why they grab it any way they can.

"Meanwhile, inwardly, what we pay our attention to and identify as our primary focus, determines our level of health and happiness. So all around that makes attention a pretty valuable asset, both inwardly and outwardly, wouldn't you say?"

Milan nodded. "I see your point about the high value of attention."

being or having?

Sukseso picked up a jasmine blossom that had fallen nearby, breathed in its fragrance, and let it fill them for a long moment. The pleasure in their cheerful face deepened. "It doesn't take much to experience a gift like this. Like I was saying, you just have to take a moment, and pay attention. Here," they said, and handed the blossom to Milan.

The technological wizard and would-be savior of the planet inhaled as well. His face instantly, helplessly relaxed and relinquished some of the seriousness of his mission, and the two sat in silence for a few moments, basking. Milan was the first to snap out of the little trance and remember why he had come. "Do you know why I'm here?" he asked.

"I can guess," Sukseso replied. "I know about your planet Ours project, and Matria also told me about your visit with her. So I assume you want to hear about how I went from Survivalism to Attentionism, correct?"

"Well, yes, that's the short version of why I'm here. But the situation is more dire than that. We have used, misused, and abused our resources and messed up Earth. Our economies are out-of-balance, unsustainable, and grossly inequitable. My plan is to colonize planet Ours and make it livable for us before Earth becomes uninhabitable. There may be beings on Ours who won't welcome us with open arms, but we can't worry about that now. The current crisis trumps all that.

"The point is, for us to succeed we need better ways of living, from all perspectives. With your expertise in business, do you think you can help us take care of our economic well-being and meet our collective needs on planet Ours without making the same mistakes we made on Earth?"

"Let me share my story with you and allow you to make that decision for yourself," Sukseso answered, settling into their cushion before they began.

"I come from a financially poor family. Growing up, money seemed to be the answer to all our problems, but we never had enough. So, as an adult I worked hard, I hustled, and I successfully and efficiently took care of this most important issue in my life and the life of my family.

"It sounds good, doesn't it? But the problem was, as a desperate child I observed and copied the habits and lifestyle of those I considered fortunate. I learned that success meant having a lot, be it money, things, or people around you. I kept increasing my possessions and the size of my companies without paying attention to other aspects of my life, like my inner world, how I felt, or how I made others feel. Remember, my focus was to be wealthy in order to resolve the one problem I knew as a child—being poor!"

"I don't understand," Milan interjected. "It sounds like you resolved it pretty well. What was the problem?"

Sukseso's smile was bittersweet: "I did, but we want and acquire things because we want to be and feel a certain way. I want this home because I want to be comfortable, to *in*-joy it. It is a state of being and feeling that we desire, even though it seems like we're chasing things. And that was the problem. I had sacrificed being free and happy in my desire for having many things.

"Every now and then I would feel on top of the world because my family, lovers, and other beneficiaries congratulated me for my achievements. But I noticed something was off. It was like sitting with someone in a restaurant and ordering what they recommended, and then your food arrives and you start eating it and realize it doesn't taste that good. But you keep pretending because there's so much fuss about it, and you've been told this is the best food here. What I didn't know was that the menu given to me was incomplete."

Milan, leaned forward, intrigued. "Incomplete? How so?"

"It lacked nutrition. And at best, it was only feeding my addiction, not my well-being." Sukseso reached for a small fig that was hanging overhead, and smiled. "Unlike this fig, one of the only ones left on the planet that has its original genes, and nutrients."

Milan's eyes widened. "Really? An organic, non-GMO fig. May I?" he asked as he reached up and pulled one down. "I haven't had one of these in *so* long. I used to eat them endlessly as a child. I *miss* them, I thought they were extinct. Which is part of the crisis we're going through." Milan bit the fruit and swooned. Afer a few long seconds, he brought the conversation back on track: "But you used a strong word, Sukseso—'addiction.' What are you talking about?"

"Well, the more I had, the more I craved. I had developed an addiction to having and doing. I think there is a disease in our modern world, I call it MMD, the More and More Disease. It's when nothing is ever enough; the more you own and do, the more you want to own and do. Not knowing that the sense of not-enough-ness comes from inside of you. Well, I had all the symptoms of MMD, but it was covered-up and praised as passion, and pursuit of success and abundance."

"That must have been confusing," Milan commented. "When did you realize you had MMD?"

"Not soon enough. Money and possessions are a thick façade for an unhealthy life. No one imagined my life was fearful or unhealthy because I owned so much. But I was racked with fear, riddled with bad habits, and ill-tempered from suffering. When I saw people who didn't work as hard as I did, I would judge and dislike them as lazy. When I saw people more successful than myself, I would dislike and envy them as lucky. It was a no-win situation. Even though outwardly it looked like I had it all, inwardly I was living in fear and lack, and quite poor, just like I was as a child."

Milan let out a small, dry laugh. "A poor child with no money, and a poor person with a lot of money—quite a story."

Sukseso sighed. "A true story. When I got sick, when my heart stopped working well, when I felt vulnerable and helpless lying in the hospital bed, I knew something had gone drastically wrong and had to change. That's when my son brought Matria to my bedside. I looked at her dubiously as she pulled up a chair, this strange woman with an old-fashioned shawl and a gentle smile. She asked how I was doing. 'Clinging to life, or so I am told,' I weakly replied. For the next hour, Matria proceeded to inform me that with all of my wealth, I had been living as a Survivalist.

"'A Survivalist,' I cried, weak as I was. That was hard to swallow. 'No way, not me! My family, maybe, but I've overcome all that. *I'm rich.* Do you know how much I own? Do you know how much I have?'

"Matria nodded that she understood. Then she asked me an interesting question. 'Facing death, when your heart nearly quit, how wealthy did you feel? How much did your possessions matter at that point?' That stopped me. Not much, I had to admit. She then said something I'll never forget. *'You have confused accumulation with abundance. They are very different things.'"*

accumulation vs. abundance

Milan was listening intently. *"Accumulation or abundance,"* he repeated. "What an interesting distinction."

"Yes, isn't it," Sukseso agreed. "I was stunned. On paper, I was abundant as could be. More so than all but a handful of people on the entire planet. But Matria was right, I didn't *feel* abundant, hence my craving to accumulate more and more.

"'How do you feel in your body when you think of all your businesses and properties and wealth?' Matria asked me.

"'My body? What body?' I moaned. I had been disconnected from my body for a long time, ever since I decided to let go of everything and focus on success.

"'First things first,' Matria said. And right there in the hospital, she led me through some exercises that reacquainted me with my arms, legs, gut, chest, head, etc. And then she asked me again, 'How does your body feel when you think of your portfolio?' My mind instantly swelled, but my body tensed up. It felt heavy, uncomfortable, tight. I felt pressure to get out of the hospital and out-do myself, to accumulate more. Then Matria said, 'Now, what does abundance feel like?'"

"Abundance?" Milan asked.

"Yes, abundance. She told me to think of a time when I felt my cup was running over, sweetly, when I had plenty of whatever it was that I treasured at the time.

"I had to stop, to really think about that one. Finally, I remembered such a time—when my first child was born. Leila, my baby girl. I felt overflowing. Like I didn't need anything more. I was so happy. All of my business cravings fell to the side. My body was light, warm, open. I wanted everyone else to feel as happy as I did. I wanted to give my joy to others, to share it. I felt like I had it all, and then some.

"Matria looked at me with a hint of a smile and asked if I felt the need to accumulate additional kids. I laughed. No, of course not, certainly not at that time. One was a world unto herself. I had no compulsive need for more.

"And suddenly, I understood. I felt the difference between accumulation and abundance. I had all of the former but none of the latter. And in that moment, as I understood the prison I was in, I felt free. That was the beginning for me, the turnaround that changed my life."

As Sukseso spoke, Milan sank into vivid memories of Kuriozi's birth, reflecting on how he had failed to savor the moment joyfully, or be fully present with his then partner, Sky. A pang of guilt and envy struck him as he compared his experience to Sukseso's moving memory of familial abundance. *Is it different for every parent, or did I miss my chance somehow?* he wondered. Catching himself drifting, Milan steered himself back to the conversation, and what he had just heard.

"That is a powerful story, Sukseso. The difference that you grasped so deeply between accumulation and abundance feels like something that could really change the way we do business on planet Ours. I mean, it's the antidote to greed, isn't it, that age-old problem that grips so many and causes such trouble in this world?"

"Precisely." Sukseso nodded. "And greed is based on the MMD, of not-enough, the accumulation of visible things to compensate for poverty inside. Whereas abundance is essentially invisible. It's what we feel when we're in love."

Milan smiled ambiguously. "*When we're in love…*" he repeated softly, as if to himself "Tell me, how did this discovery change you?"

"Oh, in so many ways," Sukseso replied. "Like I said before, when I was in accumulation mode, I compared all the time. If I saw someone who had more than me, despite my wealth I felt inferior. All the things I amassed did not help me enjoy my life more than when I didn't have them. As you said, a poor child with no money and a poor man with a lot of money—both felt the same for me."

"And abundance?"

Sukseso paused, savoring the difference. "When I saw others having more, I felt happy for them and inspired by them. I wasn't threatened. And I myself was truly happy. Abundance ended my MMD. And it gifted me with creativity and imagination. Ideas flowed naturally through inspiration, instead of forcibly through intimidation and fear. I remember exactly how Matria described the difference for me: *'Abundance is feeling certain that there are inexhaustible possibilities for creating more, and accumulation is exhaustingly demanding the production and collection of more.'* So in abundance I create, in accumulation I grind to possess. Creating frees me, possessing possesses me."

Milan smiled knowingly: "I've had those feelings, both of them. And I must admit, producing is more of a chore, while creating is like art, or play, way more fun. Okay, did this principle of abundance affect other areas of your life?"

"Yes, indeed. My suffering was mainly around the physical aspects of life, and I'm not just talking about money or success. For example, my sex life. The more the better, I thought. I went from bed to bed, person to person, experience to experience, accumulating, but I always ended up the same way—*next*! Once I shifted to abundance, I fell in love, deeply. Instead of many partners and one experience, I now have one partner and many experiences. I am not saying that this is the only way, but this felt, and still feels, perfect for me."

Love again. Milan felt a hollow ache as he listened. It had been a long time since he had been close to someone—a true partner—in love. He hadn't expected his journey to find knowledge for a better future on planet Ours to bring up old feelings he had locked up deep in the past. Or so he thought. Once again, he gently guided his attention back to Sukseso, and their talk.

"Abundance changed me in so many ways," they continued. "It facilitated my shift from Survivalism to Attentionism—I'll tell you more about that if you like. It changed the way I eat; instead of stuffing an inner sense of lack, I feed myself nutritiously for pleasure and health. Don't get me wrong," Sukseso hastened to add. "I'm still a person of appetite. But now I choose my food well, like these figs, and I love what I eat.

"I travel now in order to connect with nature, and others and myself, rather than to race around from escape to escape, or look for something I never feel I have. I relate to colleagues and friends with curiosity instead of rivalry or judgment. I think my own thoughts instead of having my frightened thoughts think me."

"What a fine distinction," Milan admired. "There's so much to discuss. But the main point is that your shift from accumulation to abundance also shifted you from Survivalism to Attentionism, right?"

"Exactly. Accumulation without end is rooted in Survivalism, the fear, as I said, of never-enough. Abundance reduced my craving and allowed me to *attend* to a bigger picture; I was free to pay attention to my inner experience, and whether my feelings, thoughts and dreams were serving me or not."

"I envy your growth, your inner growth," Milan said with feeling. "It's like you've been through a revolution in the way you experience life and the world. Abundance over accumulation is simple, but really profound, and it shows in the way you connect with others, well, at least with me. I need to think about how this can apply to planet Ours."

Sukseso bowed their head quickly and then looked warmly into Milan's eyes. "Abundance over accumulation is a breakthrough concept that applies to everything. But your main choice as an architect of a new life on a new planet is really a simple one, Milan. Once that decision is made the rest of your path will be clear."

unity by nature or unity by choice?

A harsh siren suddenly pierced the grove in which Milan and Sukseso were speaking. It was a daily disturbance that governments world-wide had adopted to safeguard people by elevating their alarm and fear. Everyone needed to be ready for the ultimate calamity, it was said. When the siren finally subsided, it gave way to the buzzing of a bee.

"And what's that simple choice?" Milan picked up.

Sukseso gazed at the bee until it lost itself quietly in a flower. They then answered Milan's question with a question: "Do you want to live separated and in the state of fear, or connected and in the state of love? This will determine how you want Ours residents to live as well. Matria says *we treat the world the way we treat ourselves, and the world treats us the way we treat ourselves too.* Living united with love is not a cute slogan developed by a PR firm. It's a true choice you have to make before you can move forward."

Milan fell into a deep silence. Minutes later, and almost embarrassed by his contemplation, he turned to Sukseso with a new question.

"I'm curious about love, but I'm equally curious about reason, thought, and the role it plays in your philosophy. You said something intriguing earlier about thinking your own thoughts instead of them thinking you. I want to know more about that."

Sukseso grinned: "Oh, I added that to my list because our relationship with our thoughts determines the nature of our relationship with anything physical. But I'm no expert in that area. I do know a great person for that discussion, though. To dive deeply into Survivalism and Attentionism from the mind perspective, you should talk to Menso. Their journey is a potent and telling one. Here is their contact info. They'll be expecting you. But now I must go. I have to be with my grandchild, who I babysit on Sundays."

Milan, startled, raised his inner eyebrow, and for a second found himself thinking ever so slightly less of Sukseso for wasting time on something they could easily hire someone else to do. *With all their talk of abundance, they babysit instead of paying for a sitter?*

Milan laughed. "You are full of surprises, Sukseso. You *babysit?*"

Sukseso was very serious as they replied, "Yes, I babysit, with immense pleasure. Being with a Little-Everything who has not yet been converted into a Something is an energetic upgrade for me. As I watch and play with my grandchild, I remember to keep many of my forgotten attributes—like curiosity, presence, and natural goodness—alive within myself. When you pay attention to young ones and connect with them deeply, you realize there is no end to their excitement for connection, and zest for exploration and expansion. What could be more abundant than that?"

With these words, and the playful bow of a child, Sukseso said goodbye. In the distance, the happy sound of their neighbors enjoying organic crops grew louder. *It must be lunchtime,* Milan thought. He was hungry too, after his long talk. But he sat where he was, sorting out the abundance of new ideas he had suddenly acquired about the meaning and feeling of success… and mulling over the blind judgmental reflex that made him think that hanging-out with kids—*kids*—could somehow be a waste of time.

3

MENSO

A
MENTAL
ATTENTIONIST
I

Milan contemplated his conversation with Sukseso for a few days, replaying it again and again in his mind. Sukseso's ideas, definitions, and ways of being in the world were all new to him, concepts he had not considered before, like being vs. having, MMD, and, most importantly, accumulation vs. abundance.

Milan was stimulated, but also provoked. Sukseso's story made him aware of missed opportunities in his own life, especially with regard to his family. *Why did I fail to nurture these relationships more consciously?* he wondered, as a newfound curiosity and self-awareness began to take root.

Milan then asked himself—is there anywhere in life that *I* have experienced accumulation and scarcity? It wasn't with money, like Sukseso. Having money was rarely a goal, just a tool to help fulfill a passion. Milan felt a sense of ease, perhaps even smugness, as he realized this.

He continued to reflect on the question for a few days, but nothing came up. Then one morning as he settled comfortably with his thoughts into his favorite chair—a womblike lambskin recliner customized exclusively for his torso—he suddenly noticed that he began to feel tense and rushed, as if he was late for a difficult meeting. He was curious about the tension in his body and the impatience in his mind that surfaced while he thought he was relaxing and feeling good. *What's going on?* he asked himself, to no avail.

Milan kept his inquiry alive and recalled what Matria had told him about the questions Attentionists ask and live by. *What's true for me in this moment? What are my wider choices beside fearful ones? What's my best choice right now?*

Many long breaths came and left before Milan found the answer to the first question—what was true for him in this moment was that he was feeling scarcity in relation to *time.* He felt he didn't have enough of it and had to rush and finish the experience at hand only to jump on to the next experience and feel rushed about that one as well. *Interesting,* he commented to himself. He would not have imagined scarcity would show up for him in such an unexpected way.

Milan's discovery brought him a sense of relief and allowed him to look for answers to Matria's other two questions: *What are my choices beyond fear? I have many, as there are all sorts of different ways to relate to time. Which is best for me right now?* Milan smiled as he chose—*Right now, in this moment, I believe befriending time is the best.*

Without delay, Milan began interacting with time in a friendly if unfamiliar fashion; no rushing, no impatience, just being present to his bodily sensations as well as his feelings. Suddenly, his chair felt softer, kinder. Milan was thrilled to find out how simply changing his question could bring about a new experience of presence and coziness. *Remarkable,* he concluded happily. *I believe in this moment what I'm feeling is abundance in relation to time.*

the topping-game!

This invigorating experience of abundance and presence added to Milan's eagerness to meet Menso and learn about their transformational experience with the mind. He arranged the meeting, and the day soon arrived.

Menso greeted Milan just as warmly as Sukseso had. They were rail thin, but glowing and wholesome, as if they drew their nourishment—and plenty of it—from unusual sources that didn't produce fat. They had thick eyebrows that bounced playfully above even thicker glasses whenever they spoke. Their home was eccentric and interesting, with walls, *all* walls, packed with books. Milan had never seen such a collection in a private home.

Midway through the 21st century no one really read books anymore, certainly not the old-fashioned, physical kind. Even virtual books were on the wane, as new chips allowed people to instantly download volumes of material—informationally, at least—in a nanosecond. Milan felt a pang of loss as he took in the colors, shapes, and age-old promise of the books before him, the promise of intimate communion, of wisdom, of a better life.

He motioned to the shelves. "Your home looks like a library, but it's so cheerful and inviting. If I had a few years, I'd move in with you and catch up on my reading."

Menso laughed, their eyebrows bobbing as they scanned the walls. "Thank you, and the old me would have proudly told you that I've read every single one of these books!"

"Well, that's no small accomplishment. Have you?"

Menso laughed again. "Almost, but it's never about what you have read or learned, as much as how and if your knowledge has raised your consciousness and affected the way you lead your life. I have to admit, that only happened for me with a few of these books."

Menso sighed, and led Milan to a table with two chairs. "Tell me how I can assist you, Milan?" they asked.

Milan got straight to the point. "I'm here because I'm desperately looking for a better way of living on another planet, as I believe we have messed up our human life on Earth and messed up Earth itself. I hear you've found ways to master your relationship with your mind, and I'm interested in seeing if your discoveries are applicable and scalable for planet Ours. I'm sure you're familiar with my plans to colonize planet Ours, and make a better life for the people of Earth on this new planet."

"Of course I've heard about your project," Menso replied. "I'll do my best to tell my story clearly, so that you can decide if it is applicable for what you have in mind."

Milan nodded appreciatively. "Let's get started then, but before we do, may I ask how you met Matria?"

"Ah, that was an early stroke of luck," Menso replied. "Matria was my teacher; she used to teach Attentionism at my junior high school. I always liked her unusual and kind teachings, and eventually that's what helped me shift from being a Survivalist to becoming an Attentionist."

Milan was almost used to Matria's terms and phrases by now, but not quite. "Can you please explain what you mean by Survivalist? I keep hearing this word but am not sure if I understand it correctly."

"Allow me to share what I believe it means through my story," Menso said.

Milan signaled for a pause, pulled out pen and paper, and prepared to take notes. After his meeting with Sukseso, he knew there would be plenty!

When he was ready, Menso began: "I come from an academic and intellectual family. We didn't care much about money or looks, but we really valued education, knowledge, the life of the mind. Being smart seemed to be the most important thing. How else could you make good decisions and avoid the bad ones that lead others astray, if not through the intelligent use of the rational, thinking mind. *Think, think, think,* was our mantra. I felt lucky to grow up in a family that understood this and passed it along."

Milan agreed. "That does sound lucky. So what was the problem?"

"For a long time, there wasn't one. Being 'a brain' worked for me in many ways. By the time I was thirty, I was brimming with knowledge and success. I went to the best schools, graduated top of the class, and rose quickly to prominence as a strategic consultant with government and private sector clients around the world. The problem was, despite my attributes and achievements, I wasn't happy. I assumed this would go away and I'd wake up one day feeling great. But I didn't. In fact, things got worse.

"The 'Topping-Game'—top school, top grades, top job, top advice—dominated my life. I corrected people all the time, either outwardly or in my head. I argued with colleagues. In my mind, we were just having a debate, but I had to win, and I usually did. People admired me and I often felt exhilarated, but not for long. I had few close friends and was increasingly stressed. I started taking pills to sleep and stimulants to wake-up. Socializing became more and more difficult. I feared others judged me as intensely as I judged them." Menso shuddered slightly while remembering.

"To stay on top I researched non-stop, watching newscasts, webcasts, forecasts, mapping the trends of the world with prototypes of not-yet-on-the-market technologies that were sent to me for testing. You could ask me anything and I could proudly tell you all about it. I was AI on two legs, with razor-sharp analytical skills, and an ongoing urge to collect as much information as possible.

"Strangely, the more critical and knowledgeable I became, the harder it was for me to make decisions. Big or small, professional or personal, everything got extremely complex. The analytic voices in my head were constantly thinking up new factors to consider. I reviewed the pros and cons of everything relentlessly. But most of the time I was stuck. Buying a car, for example, was a nightmare. It took me over a year to pick a model that I thought—but was never quite convinced—was best. Not very good for a world-class consultant to decision-makers around the globe!"

Milan conceded, "Okay, this is beginning to sound like a problem. And I can see how many of the super-intelligent mind-focused people I'll be taking to planet Ours might have similar issues. What happened next?"

inner technology

Before Menso could answer, the windows flashed with a blinding red light, followed by a blast of thunder that rocked the home and rolled down the street. Menso and Milan waited. Another red light flashed, then another. It was a common event, this eerie red lightning. Phosphorus had risen from giant fertilizer plants and farmsteads and saturated the atmosphere with a frightening and highly reactive elemental charge.

Milan looked at Menso grimly and smiled. "You see why I'm worried? Did you see the report this week predicting that red lightning would wreak unknown havoc on the planet in 3-5 years?"

Menso nodded, their voice soft and somber. "Indeed I did."

Milan shook his head. "Please, go on with your story. What happened as you were struggling to make decisions and enjoy life?"

Menso waited a few seconds before answering, to make sure the red flashes were done. "Well, I was really perplexed. I could not understand why I, with so much going for me, and such a strong and intelligent mind, was struggling. Why couldn't I find a rational solution to my emotional problems? One day, feeling lonely and depressed, I looked through some old notebooks I had written in junior high, and there I found a Matria quote from one of her classes. It said: 'Our job is to discipline our mind, care for our body, and serve our spirit.'"

Menso took a breath. "That gave me pause. I thought to my-self—well, I've disciplined my mind, so I think I got that right. But I was a little unnerved by the rest of her formula. I was rarely in touch with my body. I mean, smart people were above that, right? I had no relationship at all to my 'spirit,' whatever that was. What did Matria mean? Surely I had aced her most important requirement, the one about the mind. Nevertheless, my life wasn't all that great. Anyway, reading this quote reminded me of Matria and I went looking for her to ask for help. Maybe she had some answers that I had somehow missed.

"I was in pretty bad shape when I knocked on her door. She opened it wearing a white dress and full-length black apron full of stars, some of which sparkled and spelled out the words *Third Kind*. She was in the middle of cooking but seemed to grasp my situation at a glance. I started to explain why I had come, but before I got very far, she suggested, to my amazement, that I move in with her, take a break from my life and acquaint myself with hers."

Milan was both amused and amazed. "Just like that? She asked you to move in?"

Menso nodded, their eyebrows jumping excitedly. "Yes, but for a limited time—40 days. I know, not *that* limited! So I moved in with her with my bitten nails, strong medications, and a side-bag full of technological gadgets."

"Wow. I don't know who I'm more impressed by—you or her. So what happened at Matria's?"

Menso continued: "The first thing Matria did was ask me to put away all of my informational devices and stop checking the news. *No way*, I protested. *I need to keep up.* 'Yes, you do,' she responded. 'You need to keep up with your inner technology and the news inside.'"

Milan raised his pen: "Inner technology? The news inside? What did she mean by that?"

Menso burst out laughing. "That's what *I* asked. And she said the mind, heart, body, and spirit have vastly more complex messaging systems than anything devised by man, and they are sending out constant bulletins, many of them urgent, most of them ignored. *Tune into that!*"

Milan, was instantly intrigued. *I wonder what bulletins are shooting around inside me?* Almost immediately, a shadow clouded his thoughts, and his heart began to race as a message from his past pressed up inside him that he wasn't ready to hear or feel. *No wonder I avoid going into my inner world,* Milan thought. *Whatever this bulletin is, it's not bringing good news.*

Menso's voice momentarily came to the rescue: "I never thought there was anything newsworthy inside me either, but I quickly learned how wrong I was. Unhooked from my gadgets, inner headlines began to blare—anxiety, cravings, fear. My mind was going off non-stop.

"After a few days, things began to settle, but I was more miserable than ever. A week into my stay, sitting with Matria under a giant mulberry tree and nervously plucking the fruit, I suddenly blurted, 'Why do I feel so bad even though I'm really smart and I have it so good?'

"'That's easy,' Matria said lightly with a smile. 'You think too much.'"

Menso grimaced at the memory. "'Very funny,' I laughed. 'You're joking, right?'

"Matria shook her head. 'No, my dear. You have an over-activated and un-disciplined thinking mind.'"

ration-ality

"'A *what??*'" I cried. "As you can imagine, I was shocked. Despite all of my issues, the one problem I didn't think I had was with my thinking mind. I jumped up and declared there was no such thing as an over-active thinking mind. All of western culture agreed. I think therefore I am! Thought is intrinsically good, the more the better. I could not believe Matria was putting it down."

"I can see how that must have thrown you," Milan sympathized. "Matria herself is clearly a very thoughtful, intelligent person."

"Exactly. I got up and started pacing around the garden and said to Matria, 'Do you know my IQ? This mind that you seem to be down on is the reason I came first in the world's most prestigious schools, and advised heads of states and CEOs of Top 10 Fortune companies. How could that, of all things, be the problem?'"

Milan leaned forward: "And Matria's response?"

"Nothing. She said nothing. Instead, she eased out of her rocking chair and asked: 'Would you like to join me for a silent walk? I suggest we let go of mental activities and focus on our steps.'

"'*Whatever,*' I said to myself. I didn't want to talk to Matria at that point. She can't help me. She doesn't understand the value of the mind. I was angry, disappointed, depressed.

"We walked along a narrow stream behind her home. It took a while, but eventually my mind and emotions began to settle. My breathing slowed to the sound of the running water and I started noticing and feeling my steps, my legs, my arms. This may sound strange, but I had never paid much attention to my body, and doing so now was a surprise. *I have a body,* I thought to myself, as if discovering it for the first time. *It's nice. A little odd, but I like it.* I felt contemplative, but without a lot of thought. I noticed the trees as we walked. And the sky. I stopped and dipped my toes in the water and felt its wetness and coolness. I felt friendly towards the water, the land, the sky… and I felt an unfamiliar, reciprocal friendliness from them coming back at me.

"That evening, Matria and I ate in silence and retired to bed earlier than usual. As hard as it was for me to be silent or tolerate Matria's silence, after a while I felt a pleasant sense of spaciousness in my mind. Everything I saw as a problem was still there, but somehow I had more room to move. It was like I had been with 90 people in a small room, cramped and agitated, and now suddenly I was with them in a large field, full of yellow and green, with the sky overhead and open horizons on all sides."

Milan was impressed. "What a clear way to put it. I can imagine that."

"The next day I met Matria at breakfast. The smell of freshly baked bread greeted me, along with her wide smile. Before we ate, she bounced on a mini trampoline to wake up her body, and we both started laughing. After breakfast she told me I had a choice to continue or discontinue our discussions. She said I could stay with her for the remaining forty days and simply consider this a break from my city life. Basically, Matria left it up to me to stay as I was, or proceed with our provoking conversations and see where they led."

Menso paused, remembering the moment fondly. "I was moved by her offer and for once, without thinking over the pros and cons, I said yes. I wanted to hear what Matria had to say about my situation, no matter how challenging. I was startled and unnerved by the speed of my decision, but I let it stand."

"Did your conversations get more helpful?" Milan asked.

"More helpful yes, easier no! In fact, it got worse as Matria got more specific. When we resumed our conversation, she told me my suffering was due to the over-activation of my rational mind. Again, I lost it. 'Are you really objecting to rationality and the rational mind?' Don't forget, the way I was brought up, this was the most precious thing you could possibly have. I was already second-guessing my decision to stay, until…"

"Until what?"

"Until Matria invited me to join her in her study and look up the meaning of the word 'ration.' Frustrated, I agreed. To get to her study, we walked to the end of a long hall full of pictures of Earth and other planets, all of which seemed to have landscapes shaped like hearts. We sat down, and here's what we found:

Ration [ˈra-shən]
Restricted, scarce, allotted, divided, scattered, constricted, limited, apportioned.

"I don't know why, but somehow reading those meanings in relation to the rational mind calmed me down. I had never thought about the rational mind from the perspective of its root—*to ration*."

"Neither have I. Fascinating," Milan said.

three parts of mind

Menso nodded, still marveling at the break-through surprise of that moment. "Something shifted as I read those words. I went quiet and was able to hear Matria this time. I asked her why does our mind have to ration, divide, and limit?

"She said, 'Because this part of the mind is used by most of us most of the time, fearfully, to help us survive. It was developed in that direction when we went from being Little-Everythings to Somethings, and had to defend ourselves from other Somethings and other beings we had separated from.

"'Protection and separation are closely related. Have you seen how bodyguards protect their subjects?' Matria asked. 'They restrict them, pull them away from the crowd, stop them from connecting and mingling in order to keep them safe. This is exactly what the rational mind does in order to protect us. It is not the fault of the rational mind, it's just doing the job it was charged to do when separation and safety are involved.'"

"What an unusual explanation," Milan observed. "I've never thought of rationality that way."

"Nor had I," Menso confessed. "Anyway, I was calmer but not yet convinced. I asked Matria, 'What's wrong with the rational mind helping us survive?'

"'Nothing,'" she replied. "I am not demeaning the value of the rational mind, especially when there is a real threat. However, I am reminding you that any overdoing can turn helpful into harmful. Take good food for instance. Imagine you're hungry, you prepare a nutritional meal, and then you eat one plate, two plates, three plates, four, and you keep going. Eventually, you'll feel sick and need an intervention. The food itself was healthy, but undisciplined, excessive eating made it unhealthy.

"The same is true with the rational mind. It is absolutely necessary for it to participate—and even take charge—when our survival is truly under threat. But when it isn't and we're still relying heavily if not exclusively on it, that's when the trouble begins. Rationality of the mind is great for survival, but anxiety-riddled over-rationality is terrible for thrival!'"

Milan smiled and held up a finger to indicate another pause as he wrote down the new word. "*Thrival,* I like that. I heard Matria use this word before. She makes up lots of words. OK, what about other parts of the mind?"

"She makes up words, all right," Menso grinned. "And the next thing you know, you're using them! As for the vast and exquisite space we call mind, Matria divides it into 3 main areas; the Rational-Mind, the Whole-Mind, and an important strategic place in between: the Observation-Deck. These aspects and fields of the mind each have a spectrum and a task of their own.

"According to Matria, I was ignoring the Observation-Deck and my Whole-Mind, and instead residing full-time in a fearful corner of my Rational-Mind. That was the reason I suffered. Over-reliance on this part of my mind kept me in a chronic state of Survivalism—there's that word that you asked about—even though the dangers that I perceived everywhere, like making a bad decision about a new car or losing an argument, were hardly life-threatening and largely illusory."

Milan took a breath to process what he'd heard. "I've never thought about the different parts of the mind in this way. It always seemed like one place to me, you know, the place where thinking happened. So what happened after Matria showed you the meaning of 'ration' and explained the job of the Rational-Mind in the Survivalist state?"

the observation deck

Menso paused to clean their glasses, which had steamed up during their discourse. They put them back on their nose, smiled, and picked up where they left off. "By the time Matria and I finished our conversation, it was late and I was at capacity. I went to my room thinking if what Matria says is true, then the gift of rational thinking has turned into a beast that's destroying me from the inside. I reviewed my many stories of suffering, large and small, and began to doubt that I had disciplined my rational mind as much as it had disciplined me. Then I wondered—what is the Whole-Mind that Matria spoke about, and where the heck is the Observation-Deck? How come my educated parents and the top-notch institutions I had attended never told me about these things? As I was asking myself these questions, I fell asleep from utter weariness, and then something interesting and unexpected happened… my imagination was activated."

"Instead of your over-active thinking mind?"

Menso snapped their fingers. "Exactly. Somewhere between my dream and awake state, I imagined I was standing at Matria's so-called Observation-Deck, even though I had no idea where or what that was. The vista before me—of my mind and my life—was grand. I felt like a commander-in-chief surveying the view with full authority. There was lots of space between the things I could see and me, room to roam. My mind felt more like my domain than my demon. I could zoom in to see myself in situations, and zoom out to get a larger picture. Another intriguing thing happened; I felt the presence of a Darling friend by my side, energetically helping me and holding me throughout the night. I ended up sleeping deeply—which hadn't happened in a long time—and I got up early, refreshed and excited to see Matria and ask her more about the different parts of the mind."

"I can't wait to hear more myself," Milan chimed in. "This is really helpful, *practically* helpful, like a navigation system for the shapeless space of the mind. But, I have to ask you… *a Darling friend?*"

Menso smiled. "Matria re-told me the story of creation that I had heard many years earlier at school, including the part about the Darlings, the so-called imaginary friends who help us as we open, which I had completely forgotten about. She explained that the Whole-Mind is the part of the mind with the deeper and vaster memory and knowing. It remembers when we were Little-Everythings. It sees the whole picture of life and is connected to other wise beings, Darlings among them, as well as Big-Everything's mind."

Menso paused to see if Milan, himself a major rationalist, was having a hard time with this, but he seemed to be fine. They continued: "Matria then explained how the Whole-Mind allows us to engage the Survivalist Rational-Mind when and if needed. It includes but is not limited to it. The Whole-Mind also draws on intuition, imagination, higher rationality and wisdom. The Whole-Mind is where creation, connection and expansion take place, and what great thinkers and philosophers explored and venerated under different names in different times. This is the 'Cosmic Bank of Wisdom,' if you will—that's what Matria called it—where the ever-expanding body of collective knowing resides. And it's what you, Menso, along with many others, have confused with the over-protective rational mind.

"The Rational-Mind, however, has limited memory—it only covers the period of separation that began when we chose to live as Somethings. Its chief and automated task is protecting the self and staying alive, at least while operating—*stuck* might be a better word—in the Survivalist mode. It zooms in and magnifies problems in order to bring details to our attention.

"Unfortunately, when over-activated, it over-magnifies and over-focuses on too many details, relevant or not. It's like watching an ant under a microscope and seeing Godzilla. This makes it hard for us to discern a true danger from an exaggerated or fabricated one. It also makes it hard to turn off the reactionary switch of attack and defend."

"Extraordinary," Milan declared, surprised by how intriguing he found Menso's and Matria's ideas. "I like how you're hooking up the parts of the mind with Matria's story of creation, you know, Somethings and Little-Everythings. What about the Observation-Deck?"

Menso drew a breath and continued: "The Observation-Deck, for an Attentionist, is a really exciting part of the mind. It allows us to zoom out and see the vaster picture of what's going on in the present moment, and hence see the wider options and potential solutions. This is where we come to balance the mind and be present with and curious about our choices. Without going here, we get lost in problems, and our habitual, historical, sometimes hysterical way of reacting to them. Remember Matria's three Attentionist questions? What are the facts? What are my choices? And what is my best choice? Standing here makes it easy for us to find answers to those questions.

"Choice does exist in the Rational-Mind at the level of Survivalism, but it is limited to survival choices that don't have much to do with what comes beyond survival. In other words, thriving and being happy."

Menso cleared their throat. "To get back to your earlier question, Milan, Survivalists are the Somethings that live in fear because they have forgotten their Everything-ness, their powerfulness, and their togetherness. They see every situation and every being as a problem and a danger. They ignore the potentiality and opportunities of life. They are stuck in the rational mind.

"Attentionists, on the other hand, are Little-Everythings-in-training, with choice-consciousness and access to both the worlds of Somethings and Little-Everythings. They live in choice, and travel between various parts of the mind as needed with no restriction or obsession, and with intentional attention. They have a high AQ, as Matria calls it, and hence see many options at each choice-point in their lives, be it small, medium, or large."

"Options are good. We all need options," Milan said, and felt.

Menso vigorously agreed. "These insights floored me. Just imagining the Observation-Deck provided me with relief that night at Matria's. It was a place that, with all of my education and high IQ, I had no idea existed. While I was busy following my familial and familiar mind-map of knowledge, I had completely forgotten my inner-map of knowing."

knowledge vs knowing

Milan clapped his hands together. "Menso, you're on a roll. What's the difference between knowledge and knowing?"

Even through their heavy lenses, Menso's eyes were shining: "Knowledge is what we obtain by learning and gathering information, and making the most of experience. Knowing is what we access by allowing our deeper and higher self to come through. Knowing is a much larger and deeper insight that goes beyond personal or acquired knowledge. It's available to all of us, when and if we choose to access it. It's what we all knew how to access as Little-Everythings, when we shared our pool of knowledge along with an ocean of knowing. It is the collective knowledge of all times, where insights and unlearned wisdom come from. Knowing is the universal savings account, available for our withdrawal, at the Cosmic Bank of Wisdom, where all elevated beings deposit their learnings."

Milan couldn't help but smile at the notion of a cosmic bank full of knowing. "What a fine distinction," he said. "I've never heard that before. The way you put it, knowing seems more valuable than knowledge."

"In choice, there is room for both," Menso clarified. "The challenge starts when in fear and running we limit ourselves to knowledge and don't make room for knowing."

Milan repeated "*knowledge, knowing*" a few times, trying to memorize the distinction. As he did, his ring buzzed with the arrival of a message. He ignored the first and second alerts, but on the third, he checked. It was his office, pressing him about an urgent matter.

"I have to go," he told Menso. "Can we pick this up tomorrow?"

Menso agreed, and their conversation came to an unexpected end.

MENSO

A MENTAL ATTENTIONIST II

Menso took the afternoon off to go slow, enjoy the rest of the day, and do as they pleased. They sat on their balcony under the sun and immersed themself in the world of trees that surrounded their home. *Nature is the greatest book of all,* they said quietly with a smile. *Inexhaustible.* They wondered what wisdom of interconnection the trees might hold. What did they know about supporting each other and other living things, in the air and in the ground, that Menso didn't know, or had forgotten?

Milan, on the other hand, rushed to the rescue of his team, driving past trees that disappeared in a blur, wisdom and all. Nevertheless, he came back fresh and curious the following day.

"Is everything okay?" Menso asked as they sat down and resumed their talk.

"Yes, all is well now," Milan replied. "But if my talented, intelligent team members could learn to use their imagination a bit more, things would get much easier for them and for me. On that note, may I ask you what Matria says about imagination? I was wondering about that on my way over, especially in relation to Attentionism."

"Good question, Milan. For an Attentionist, imagination is a valuable tool. Matria says imagination is the formation of new ideas, images, or concepts not present to the senses. But it needs to be love-based. Not all imaginations have newness and/or are loved-based, and therefore..."

"Wait a minute," interrupted Milan. "You lost me here."

Menso smiled as their eyebrows danced. "Let me explain. Take worrying, for instance, which is a kind of imagination. Meaning the mind is making up images and ideas that are not present in that moment. Generally, they're based on a difficult past or a feared future, unless you're worrying about a real and current problem.

But even then, the mind makes up images/ideas/concepts that may be new in form, but old in essence, and based on fear.

"Research shows that eighty-five percent of the things we worry about never come to pass. That's why I say worry is imagination, and that it's old and fear-based. Of course, there's always true worrying that alerts us to a risk we need to pay attention to, but I'm referring to the kind of unnecessary and unhelpful patterns of worry that for instance I was producing in my mind before I reconnected with Matria. The imagination that has helped me and other Attentionists create new options has a different essence and result. It gives life, energy and image to a new and love-based way of being, doing, and having, which adds to our wellbeing, not our misery."

"So, worrying is imagination gone fearfully wrong?" Milan asked.

"Precisely. And imagination is thinking gone lovingly infinite!"

Milan leaned back and repeated: "*Worrying is imagination gone fearfully wrong, imagination is thinking gone lovingly infinite.* Now this is worth noting and taking to Ours. I had never considered worry as a kind of imagination, but you're right; if it's not happening and my mind is making it up, then it's clearly imaginary."

"Right! And the way you use your imagination—to worry or to dream—depends on whether you're a mental Survivalist or a mental Attentionist."

"A mental Attentionist—I definitely want to hear more about that. But before I forget, I have another question about the Rational-Mind. If its main function for most people most of the time is to help us survive, why do we revere it so much when survival isn't really an issue anymore?"

"Habit. Conditioning. Addiction, if you will," Menso replied. "Matria says that when Somethings changed their story from unity to separation, they became denser and tenser, and created a history of fear that gave prominence to survival and consequently the rational mind, or at least a certain way of using the rational mind.

"She points to an ancient Persian saying that salt is used to preserve things, but what do you do when the salt itself starts to rot? The same story applies here: what do we do when the rational mind, which is supposed to protect us from outside dangers, moves in and becomes a danger itself?"

survivalism and the rational mind

Milan went quiet as he reviewed his own pattern of mind. What was his relationship with his rational mind? Was he also living in survival mode? *Maybe in my family life,* he ruminated, *where I've kept a few things under lock and key? And for good reason,* he hastened to assure himself. Then smiled at his words. *Maybe "reason," and fear, have made me a Survivalist in other areas as well.*

Menso sat in silence as they watched Milan traveling in his mind. They loved standing at the Observation-Deck, taking in the various views, both inner and outer. They felt free to have fun like a kid, letting their awareness go wide and far, from field to field, from new images and colors to new geometries and numbers. They came back to the room when Milan asked another question.

"Menso, I hear what you're saying about over-using one aspect of the Rational-Mind, but how does an Attentionist benefit from the Rational-Mind, meaning what is the role of the Rational-Mind in the Attentionist world?"

"An Attentionist's Rational-Mind is not addicted to questions of survival and spends its energy exploring and figuring things out.

The Rational-Mind loves to do that. We need the Rational-Mind, and it's fun working with it, as long as we're not panicked by it."

"Of course," Milan mused, "the Rational-Mind figures things out. That makes sense."

"Yes, the Rational-Mind is a fantastic figure-outer," Menso continued. "That's how we solve puzzles, find solutions, and expand our knowledge of inner and outer life. In fact, it's exciting to invite our Rational-Mind to play with us in these fields. Fear and excitement carry the same level of energy, except one from a place of no-choice, and the other from choice."

"So when we use our Rational-Mind to figure out things with excitement, we're not in survival mode?" Milan asked.

"What do you think? Go back to when you enjoyed solving a problem for your projects or your personal life and tell me what state you were in."

Milan closed his eyes and recalled the exciting times he had when he arrived at a clear decision, a new idea, an invention. He loved that feeling. It's when he felt most receptive, abundant, alive.

"Ok, you're right," he conceded happily, "that's not survival mode. But how then do we know when we are stuck in survival?"

"There are many ways, but for me the best indicator is when I feel tense and contracted in my body." Menso shifted slowly in their chair, as if spurred by their own comment to check themselves out. "Bio-feedback, remember that phrase? It's real. But I also pay attention to when I hear myself generalizing, catastrophizing, personalizing, eternalizing, dramatizing. When my only connection with my heart is through challenging feelings. When my rating of the importance of a topic, and how I'm handling it, don't match. In short, when my suffering is greater than my pain and gain, I know I'm in survival mode."

"And when your suffering is greater than your pain and gain, what do you do then?"

"What helps me the most is looking for and finding something to love in the midst of my pain; a painting, a tree, a geometric shape or color, another being, anything really. The idea is to go from fear to love, the subject is irrelevant. If I can't find anything or anyone to love, then I use my physiology to change my state of mind.

"I might put my face in ice water, smile, whistle, hum, slow down my breathing, laugh, or even yawn. These physical actions send a signal to my frightened mind that all is well and there's no need for protection in that moment."

Milan made a face: "Ice water? Smiling, whistling, humming, yawning… seriously? Does that really help?"

"Indeed it does, Milan. Indeed it does. Basically it tells my mind to snap out of it, or to relax. To know that all is well and there is no need for protection in this moment.

"And then, gently, after calming my mind, I go to the Observation-Deck and ask myself what other choices I have beside what my frightened Rational-Mind is offering me right now? You see, sooner or later we all might end up on the Observation-Deck, using our Whole-Mind to connect with our deeper knowing. The question is can we go there voluntarily and intentionally for gain, or do we have to be pushed there through pain and difficult events. It's a question of freedom, and how intentional we are."

visitor's visa to future and past

Milan sighed: "It's true, something bad usually has to happen to force us into alternatives, or onto the Observation-Deck, as you call it. The key point here is that you're managing your attention, right? But how?"

"That is indeed the key point, Milan, and the challenge. As an Attentionist, I'm frugal with my attention; I pay it to those things that add to my well-being, and take it away from those which reduce it. Here's a secret that might be helpful to people on Ours—we can only access our intentional attention—as opposed to our undisciplined wandering attention—in the present moment. Which means that practicing presence is an effective way to go from survival to choice. Getting lost in the past or the future takes away our ability to choose."

Milan wriggled in his chair and made a face: "I always feel uncomfortable with this emphasis on the present. Please don't tell me our past is useless or our future not worth imagining or planning," he said.

"Oh, no, not at all," Menso cheerfully replied. "We need the lessons of the past and flexible planning for our future, and I regularly visit them both. But I do so while staying anchored in the present. I imagine I have a short-term visitor's visa to go to the country of the past with an itinerary of learning and growing. I go there as an Attentionist, observe, pick and choose souvenir lessons that serve me, and then leave before my visa expires. I know over-staying as a Survivalist will bring nothing but lamenting and suffering.

"Same with the future, I go there with an itinerary of gently planning. I explore possibilities, let myself dream, research as needed, draft a plan, and again, before my visa expires, return home to the present moment to access my knowing. Then, working with my knowledge and my knowing, I make the best plan available to me at that moment. Going to the country of the future as a curious Attentionist is very different than getting stuck there as an anxious Survivalist!"

Milan was impressed by Menso's visa analogy. He marveled at the simplicity of it, and how helpful it could be in an area that he found difficult, especially in relation to his past. "Your journey is remarkable, Menso. Had you known all that you know now, do you think you would have pursued the same field?"

Menso smiled brightly. "Probably, yes, but not with the same troubled energy and at such a high price. You see, it's not so much what we do in life, as how and in what state we do it. Doing my best, becoming an authority, learning a lot, was not the problem. The problem was doing all that in a state of intense, largely unconscious and normalized fear, while suffering mentally. As Sukseso would say, I was living in a state of accumulation instead of abundance, the only difference was the things I collected were knowledge, information, and strategies. I relied exclusively on knowledge, and not at all on knowing. On the Rational-Mind without any awareness of the Observation-Deck or Whole-Mind. These were my problems, not my line of work."

emotions and thoughts

Milan and Menso sat silently for some time, letting the conversation settle. The walls of books, with their many shapes and colors and collective aura of knowledge and truth, seemed to hold and support their exchange, like friends.

Milan was the first to speak: "I'm hesitant to ask another big question, as I have already gotten so much from our conversation, but I must. You mentioned suffering, Menso. As a mental Attentionist and an expert on the mind, what's the relationship between emotion and thought? Sometimes it seems like it doesn't matter what or how we think, our emotions are so strong."

Menso laughed, holding up one of their long fingers: "Ah, the famous 'last question' trick. You're opening up a whole new world with this one, Milan. I'm happy to go there with you, but you'll need to buckle up for the ride."

"I'm already on-board. Let's go."

"Our thoughts are electric and our emotions are magnetic," Menso said, pausing for a moment to let their words register before continuing. "When you think of something you create electricity. When you feel it, a magnetic energy is born. Thinking and feeling about the same subject creates an electro-magnetic charge that has both a strong energetic force and power of attraction.

"Are you with me, Milan? Helpful, love-based thoughts and emotions generate an unstoppable drive in a positive direction. Weakening, fear-based thoughts and emotions either stop us in our tracks or take us the other way. Eventually, we learn to integrate our thoughts and emotions and to think and feel intentionally. Instead of our thoughts thinking us, or our emotions pushing us, we are in charge."

"Quite a theory," Milan declared. "I'm not sure I fully understand it, but I am sure that managing our emotions is critical to life on Earth, or Ours, and I want to learn more."

"Oh, for that you have to speak with my dear friend and collaborator, Lamenti. They know this area best and can shed a much brighter light on the topic of emotions and Attentionism."

"Wow. Another Attentionist in the neighborhood," Milan said with a laugh. "How many of you are there? But seriously, before I leave, Menso, any last words for me and planet Ours?"

Menso mulled the question before answering: "We have many names for our unhealthy mental states, but the only true disease of the mind in my view is the disease of separation. We suffer because we have a Survivalist filter that receives and translates things and people as hazardous, even when they are not. In that mindset, well, the mind is *set*. Meaning it's hard to get to the Observation-Deck or the Whole-Mind, and there is no room for flexibility, perspective, wholeness or growth. Like I said, the problem resides within, when we're not really in danger, even though we think and feel that we are.

"As for moving to another planet, the challenge is not Earth and what we have done to it, even though we have damaged it greatly. Earth is a living, breathing, conscious being, just like us. It can repair itself brilliantly when it is ready to do so and we can help it by repairing our own separated suffering selves. The problem is the way we live on Earth. As you have said, unless we change that, we'll take it with us wherever we go. It's not necessarily planets we need to change, it's the relationship with our mind, our emotions, and other beings, all beings, that needs to evolve.

"That said, I hope my story can help Rational-Mind Survivalists no matter where they live. I really enjoyed your visits Milan, but I have to leave now and go to a Silent Party with my friends."

"Excuse me, Menso—did you say 'Silent Party?'" Milan asked, with a bemused look.

"I did indeed," Menso playfully replied, "My friends, curious guests, and I get together every month for this. We communicate energetically; we eat, dance, laugh, play music—all without words. This allows us to connect with the 'inner technology' and deeper knowing that we usually ignore. It's a gift and a break from our word-filled world of socializing. And it's a great practice for going to the Observation-Deck in a communal setting."

Milan smiled, with a hint of an eye-roll that suggested he thought Menso's idea of fun was a little off-kilter. "I can't fathom a party without words, and I don't think I'd enjoy one," he said, as if contemplating something bizarre and unpleasant to eat.

Menso was cheerfully unfazed: "You'd be amazed to see what happens when politics and fear of correct words are removed from our interactions. In silence, attention—and intention—are rescued. We can hear our loud mind adjust its voice and arrive at an integrated place of mind and heart."

"That's a big promise for a small party, isn't it?"

"Which part of your mind is asking this question, my friend?"

"Ok, perhaps my Survivalist mind."

"May I invite you to join us once, experience silence in the midst of a crowd, and then we can speak from the point of experience?"

Milan grimaced, playfully. "Fair enough."

"Often the Survivalist mind and its made-up questions stop us from experiencing new ways. Join us next month. You never know, silence may be more interesting—and revealing—than you think."

"Yes, that's the part that worries me," Milan grumbled, as Menso said goodbye and left the room.

5

LAMENTI, AN EMOTIONAL ATTENTIONIST

I

Alone at Menso's, surrounded by walls teeming with books and his own mind teeming with new and exciting ideas, Milan reviewed the highlights of their conversation: the importance of "inner technology;" obtaining a "visa" to go to the past and/or future; separation as a disease of the mind; the difference between knowledge and knowing; and, most importantly, the roles of the Rational-Mind, the Whole-Mind and the Observation-Deck. Plus, of course, the Silent Party, which Milan, despite himself, was curious to try out.

Milan wondered if/how mental Survivalism had shaped his life. He realized that he hadn't truly reflected on or learned from his past, nor had he explored his mind's Observation-Deck, at least not in relation to some intensely difficult and personal areas. Memories of Sky and Kuriozi became more vivid in his heart, even as he pondered the state of his mind. *Will I ever access my Whole-Mind when it comes to Kuriozi and Sky?*

The next day, something unexpected happened. Milan met with his planet Ours team to provide feedback on their latest research and recommendations. He was not fully satisfied with their report, and the main presenter asked him to elaborate. Milan replied, there's something missing. The presenter said, what do you think is missing? Milan found himself uttering the following words: This does not feel right or complete. *The findings and recommendations are purely from the point of view of the Rational-Mind, not the Whole-Mind.*

Milan's statement surprised him more than his team. To be sure, his team members felt lost and asked him to elaborate, to which Milan replied: "We need to look at this from a higher and larger point of view. A limited, merely rational view may be necessary at times, but in this case it doesn't give us all the options." Then he skillfully invited everyone to come along with him, symbolically speaking, and survey the data from the Observation-Deck, where they could see much much more. The team got it, and Milan felt comfortable illustrating his point. He realized the language may have been foreign to his team, but the path was easy enough for them to follow.

That night, as Milan returned home, he realized he unknowingly visited the Observation-Deck and used the Whole-Mind from time to time. But now he had a name and address that allowed him to go there quickly, navigate various zones of his mind, and benefit from all aspects of it more often and more intentionally.

The next morning he thought to himself *I may be good at the mind stuff, but emotions are a language I'm not fluent in.* He wondered how the next Attentionist would unfold that world for him. So he contacted Lamenti and arranged his next rendezvous.

lamenti's lament

Lamenti's home was a bit far, but Milan didn't mind the drive. It was scenic and relaxing, except for a platoon of small surveillance drones that suddenly appeared overhead. The government had announced a heightened alert for dirty bombs after a number of cities had suffered radioactive attacks. Drones were now a daily occurrence, darting in all directions, scanning whole neighborhoods for traces of nuclear material, or physiological signatures known as "Orca pheromones." Experts claimed the sophisticated bio-markers could identify someone planning an attack. But there were many mistakes and raids that ended tragically.

The question of time is a real one, for the planet at least, Milan thought gloomily as he drove out of the swarm. *How much of it do we actually have?*

He arrived at Lamenti's home earlier than planned. To his surprise, Lamenti was waiting at the door, as if expecting him. They had a strikingly gentle face, with bright eyes and skin that hung sleekly off their cheeks, as if they had once been bulging but now were utterly relaxed. They wore soft linen pants and a white shirt with loose, long sleeves that billowed whenever they waved their arms, which was often.

Lamenti's simple yet brightly decorated home was full of paintings with lots of red, yellow, blue, and green that immediately cheered Milan up. The colors were both calming and energizing, and as he took them in Lamenti poured some tea, a beautiful golden brew made of saffron that added another hue to the occasion. Milan enjoyed a few sips and then got to the point. "Thank you for meeting with me, Lamenti. Let me tell you why I'm here."

"Please do. I think I know why—the whole world is getting to know about your mission to Ours—but I'm eager to hear about it from you."

"The way we human beings have lived so far has ruined the planet," Milan stated flatly. "The situation is critical, much more than most imagine, and I'm determined to do something about it. I'm gathering information, expertise, and now wisdom, to take to planet Ours. Because not only do I want to give us all a fresh start, I want to make sure we don't repeat the mistakes of Earth in our new home. We're heading for destruction, and the sad part is we either don't know or don't care. I want to create a superior, sustainable life on planet Ours."

"A grim but accurate picture, but with a dash of hope," Lamenti concurred. "How may I help?"

"Well, emotions seem to have a lot to do with the dire situation we're in. That is to say, our inability to handle them. Can you tell me the story of your emotional life? I'm hoping it will provide some insights that will help us on Ours."

"Of course, Milan." Lamenti closed their eyes, lifted their willowy, loosely covered arms, and let them settle slowly, like scarves. They then smiled and began: "My story is not unusual, though it may sound extreme. I come from an emotionally impaired family. There was a lot of drama and trauma in our household. Both of my parents and two grandparents were diagnosed with mood disorders. Rage and tears were common, especially from those 'in charge.' But we covered everything up and pretended all was well. I was taught to deny my emotions and put a happy face on everything, all the time.

"As a young adult I felt fragile, frightened, angry, and most of all, shortchanged. I felt like I had no voice. I didn't know how to express my feelings at all. In my heart, I was begging my family and friends—*someone, please, ask me how I feel*—but when I spoke, I minimized my problems and exaggerated or made up positive experiences. I pretended I was the luckiest person around and was praised for being such an agreeable individual and a rock to so many. I was a rock alright, emotionally blocked and sinking fast."

"Did you seek professional help?" Milan asked.

"I sure did. As soon I reached adulthood, and that's when I began to understand what had happened to me, how crazy my home environment was, and how stifled I had become."

Lamenti paused again as they remembered. "The deep, long, psychological work I did finally allowed me to identify and feel my emotions, find my voice and let people know how I felt. At first, my strongest emotion was fear, but eventually that gave way to anger about what had happened to me and against those responsible. And boy did I let it out. It felt good to finally stand up for myself, meet fire with fire, and break the conspiracy of silence that had caused so much suffering and pain."

"That sounds like real progress," Milan offered.

"It was, but progress at one level may not be enough at another."

"I'm not sure what you mean by that, but please go ahead with your story."

"Well, people said I complained a lot. In my mind, I was telling the truth, calling out my father for his rage, my mother for her hysterics, and my other relatives for their complicity in the repressed, hush-up culture that we called home. I thought, someone needs to tell these people what's wrong with them, and I am pissed off enough to do it. I was determined to get the anger out."

"Do you believe this was your emotional break-through?"

"No, this was what led me to my emotional *break-down*."

"Really? Why? What happened?"

matria and lamenti

Lamenti leaned back in their chair and looked upward for a few seconds, as if watching a movie on a faraway screen. Then they began.

"Well, I had broken out of my family prison, but I was still miserable. I felt victimized by my upbringing and genes. My story was so heavy and real that it seemed like I didn't have a chance. Despite my progress, I had a hard time relating to others. I often over-reacted to things they said and did. I had a lot of buttons and triggers. Worst of all, the anger that I tried so hard to get out of my system seemed inexhaustible and was getting stronger. I felt like I had every right to feel it, of course, and my practice of letting people know how I felt continued. I railed regularly. But then, one night, I lost it completely.

"On the eve of a new year, to feel good, I invited family members, friends, and a few colleagues to my home to celebrate. Things were going pretty well until my mom made a comment about me while we were all in the kitchen helping to clean-up. One of my colleagues asked me a question about my childhood and as I started to answer, my mother jumped in and said this is not the place or time for your childhood memories, dear. That one comment threw me off an emotional cliff."

Lamenti's arms began to jump and flail. "I started screaming at my mom and throwing things around. I cursed and accused. I shared the details of our family story with the whole gathering. I was in an altered state of rage. No one moved, said anything, or even tried to stop me. Suddenly the phone rang. I had screamed so loudly that my neighbor, Matria, heard me from her home next door and called.

"Matria and I had lived next to each other for years, but she had never called before. I didn't even know she had my number. She was teaching at a school nearby, and I had come across her from time to time, but honestly, she looked too happy for my comfort at that stage of my life, and I never went beyond saying hello."

Milan felt some discomfort and judgment about Lamenti's emotional wildness and gloom, but his interest in their story was strong. "What did she say when she called?"

"She said she just wanted to wish me a happy new year, and that she loved New Year's Eve because of how powerful new beginnings could be. It was a short call. When we hung up there was a heavy silence in the room. A bit later the doorbell rang. It was just before midnight. I thought, oh no, crazy happy Matria has called the police. I ordered everyone to stillness and opened the door, ready to attack or defend as needed."

"What did the police say?"

"She had not called the police. The person at the door was Matria herself, with a large basket of fruits from her garden and some cookies she had baked. She walked right in without an invitation, and started serving them to everyone. She told us that eating her handpicked fruits and handmade cookies would help us start the new year with great energy. She was warm and intentional and we desperately needed a break from the awkward situation I had created. So my family members pretended all was well, as was our tradition, and my guests treated Matria as a welcomed intruder who brought a sense of celebration to the room."

"What a way to end the year," Milan shuddered. "What happened to your guests, did they stay for the New Year?"

"Everyone stayed and we all ate Matria's tasty treats, hugging and kissing as if nothing had happened. My guests jumped up and down at the twelfth hour, while I asked myself *who is this Matria*? How did she end up in my house at midnight with so much energetic influence, knowing exactly what to do to at least partly thaw the frozen air I had created. We celebrated with a sense of awkward happiness, and my guests left together shortly afterward; I don't think anyone wanted to be the last one alone with me. Later that night I went to bed depleted and humiliated. I felt I had ruptured my stature socially, professionally and within my family, all in one night."

the triangle of choice

Milan recalled his own emotional turmoil after discovering Sky's affair with her music teacher. Not a physical affair, but an "intimate" one, as she put it. He too had "lost it" completely. Even now, ten years later, he rarely let himself think about this, and for good reason; it took him to a dark and unbearably painful place. Noticing Lamenti's gaze, Milan collected himself and returned to the conversation.

"What a meltdown, Lamenti. How did you recover from this?"

"I didn't. I isolated myself for a while. I felt embarrassed and unready to go back to work. I was an attorney and spent my days pleading on behalf of others, but now I couldn't face my colleagues and my team. I had a feeling everyone was talking about me. I decided to take some time off. I don't know why but I wanted to see Matria again. I wanted to come clean about what had happened that night. I somehow felt comfortable speaking to her and had a feeling she might be able to help me. Long story short, I knocked on her door. She answered sweetly, as if she was expecting me, and I ended up staying with her for the next few weeks."

"That's amazing," Milan said, with a shake of the head. "Menso told me a similar story of Matria inviting them in for 40 days. Who does that? It sounds like you finally found someone you could confide in."

"Well, yes, but not for long. At first it was great to share my personal and family history with Matria. She was a deep listener and I felt heard and seen. But things shifted when I asked her if she had any wisdom to share about my situation.

"Matria was silent for a moment. Then she asked me what *my* role was in creating my challenging life. I was startled. I told her again how difficult and emotionally challenging life had been for me. It wasn't my fault that I was unlucky, I said. I was given a bad hand, genetically and historically."

"Did Matria agree with that?" Milan asked. "Did she retract or revise her question?"

"No retraction and no revision. 'Lamenti,' she said, 'it is not about fault or luck, it's about responsibility and choice.'"

"But what about nature and nurture, what you inherit and how you grow up?" Milan pressed. "Doesn't Matria believe in that?"

"I asked that question too, only *I* asked it with a lot of anger. To which Matria answered: 'There is a triangle with three elements that make us who and how we are—our genes, our history, and our choice. Most animals and plants come to this world a certain way and leave the same. They are led by their instinctual behaviors and biological processes of genes, plus their history on Earth, not conscious decision-making.

"'A human being, however, can choose to activate, moderate, or even deactivate the expression of their genes by the conscious choices they make. They can use their personal history like a canvas with some paint on it, as a starting point that lets them work with what's already there, and at the same time create something new and unique. It's challenging, but very rewarding when an artist turns unwanted colors and shapes into their own piece of art.

"'That is what wise people do. They find ways to turn poison into medicine by awakening their choice-consciousness and activating their choice-authority. choice is what distinguishes humans from other beings without choice.'"

"Choice-consciousness, choice-authority," Milan slowly repeated, as if enjoying the sound of the words. "That's certainly an empowering way of looking at things. Was Matria's explanation convincing for you?"

"To a point. I found her triangle of genes, history and choice intriguing and helpful, and I was happy that she was promoting 'choice-consciousness,' but I also found it frustrating. Had she not been listening to me? Surely she saw that I, of all people, had become a strong choice-maker. I had found my voice and chosen to use it, loudly, firmly, again and again and again. I was an activist in breaking silences, expressing myself, and helping others do the same. I was already exercising my choice. The more Matria explained, the angrier I felt. How could she not see and appreciate my progress?"

"Yes, you had certainly come a long way," Milan sympathized. "And I can imagine future residents of Ours bringing emotional wounds not unlike yours to the new world. Did Matria accept that you were already a choice-maker?"

"Yes, she did… but she said I was making choices *as a* Survivalist. That stopped me cold."

survivalists, attentionists and emotions

"*Making choices as a Survivalist*—what a startling idea," Milan declared.

"I know. It was the first time I heard that word. Matria then explained the 3 states of being—Survivalism, Attentionism, and Eternalism. She told me Survivalists have limited choices; at best they survive, but they don't get to move beyond survival into what she calls 'thrival.' Matria said a chronic complainer or reactive person cannot be a true choice-maker the way an Attentionist can."

"Hey, wait a minute," Milan interrupted. "*I* complain, and it never stopped me from choosing… I don't think. I want to come back to this. But tell me, how else do Survivalists and Attentionists work differently with their emotions?"

"Well," Lamenti continued, "Survivalists act out their emotions and Attentionists feel them out, literally, in their bodies, but also as a way of choosing and changing the feelings they want to have. Matria explained that even though we use the words 'emotions' and 'feelings' interchangeably, they are different in their nature.

"Feelings are our foundational, natural, healthy states of well-being, like joy, balance, and connection. Emotions are transient energies that move through us in order to inform us how near or far we are from the feelings we really want to have.

"It's like the Hot & Cold game we used to play as kids. Emotions are like a bell that lets us know where we are in relation to where we want to be. The more unpleasant and unwanted the emotion, the louder the bell and the further we are from feeling good, i.e. safe, happy, loved.

"When we hold on to difficult emotions as a complainer, we don't let them do their job—inform us and move on. We make them more long-term than they're designed to be. But there is no place for them to stay in us, and that's why we eventually act or throw them out, often in unhealthy ways. Our emotions are meant to be visitors, not residents. Informers, not companions.

"Making uncomfortable but impermanent emotions and energies permanent keeps us from experiencing our desired core-feelings of wellbeing. I have to add, as much as Matria sees complaining as an unhealthy state, she is all for *venting,* which allows us to express, share, unfold and clear out our emotions for the purpose of moving forward toward wellbeing. So long as we don't vent as a way of abusing someone else."

"Agreed," Milan said. "I've been around some bad venting, and that's never good. I'm really intrigued by Matria's analysis of feelings and emotions and their relationship. I'm eager to test it out on some of my own feelings and emotions when we're done."

"But wait, there's more!" Lamenti added with a laugh. "When we tune into our emotions and allow them to be tools that clarify what we truly seek, we can then set and guide our intention and attention, and give birth to helpful action. Fluid and flowing intention, attention, and action, instead of rigid reaction."

Milan put up a hand for Lamenti to pause: "Let me see if I got this right. First you feel out your emotions in your body. Then, if you wish, you vent out safely to yourself or someone else who says it's ok, which helps you clarify the feeling you're really after. That then makes it possible for you to have clear intention, focused attention, and wise action, all of which gets you closer to your desired feeling?"

"Well put, Milan—clear intention, focused attention, and wise action."

"Okay. What if I emote comfortable emotions? Does that mean I'm already feeling what I desire to feel?" Milan asked.

"Correct. Like right now, I'm feeling connected, safe, and heard. So my emotions are pleasant even though I'm speaking about difficult memories. They're telling me as far as feelings are concerned, I'm in my desired place."

an emotional beggar?

Milan smiled warmly: "And I'm feeling stimulated and happy even though we're talking about the crisis of humanity and the whole frigging planet. I too must be in my desired place. So what happened next?"

"Well," Lamenti proceeded, "Matria's distinctions about feelings vs. emotions, feeling out vs. acting out, and complaining vs. venting, gave me a lot to think about. And I was about to thank her for taking me further on my journey of growth. But then she said something that I just could not handle: 'My dear,' she said, 'you have grown a lot, but emotionally speaking, you are a beggar.'

"That word, *beggar*, shocked me, triggered me, sent me right back to how I was on that dreadful night. I mean, I lost it again, and this time I lost it with Matria."

Lamenti's cheeks bulged all-out like balloons, stayed taut for a few moments, then slowly relaxed. "I said, do you really think I am a beggar? I *used* to be a beggar with no voice, but I have changed so much. Did you not hear me screaming at everyone that night? Everyone was petrified and silenced by me. Do you even know what begging means?"

"I have to say," Milan interjected, "if you are an emotional beggar, then so are most of the powerful people I know, including myself. They, I, we lose it often."

"Wait 'til you hear more, Milan. Matria brought her voice down as if she was about to share a secret with me. 'Begging has many different styles and sounds, from crying, to silence, to yelling, to threatening—even to violence. In essence, as long as we expect, demand, or wait for others to change in order for us to feel different, whole, happy, or well, we are—fundamentally—begging. We are held hostage to our own reactivity and someone else's unwillingness or inability to behave the way we would like.

"'*You*, Lamenti, are begging emotionally, not because you have a meek, beggarly voice, but because you are living an un-free emotional life. You've been waiting all your life for family members, friends, partners, neighbors, colleagues to be different in order for you to feel good and happy. Anyone can and many do provoke you and determine your emotional state. Anyone, *except you*. You have confused forceful with powerful, pleading with requesting, yelling with commanding."

"Wow, *wow*… apparently so have I, Lamenti. Especially the yelling part!"

Saying this, Milan thought about his occasional outbursts at work. That didn't bother him too much. For one thing, he didn't think he was begging. Plus, he thought he had the right, being, well, *Milan*. But then another memory popped up and his blood ran cold. *How I yelled when Sky told me she couldn't feel me anymore, that I was emotionally cut off and she was thinking of leaving. I couldn't believe it. All I could do was scream. And then shut down. With her, with Kuriozi, with everyone.* Milan felt a shiver run up his spine. *What was I doing? What have I done? How can I recover from these outbursts, and the damage they have caused?*

Sensing that the conversation had triggered something in Milan, Lamenti waited, then caught his eyes before starting again.

"Begging, however it shows up, is a real problem—for you, me, and most of us on planet Earth. Matria's words landed like a dagger in my heart. They rang true, even though they hurt a lot. Anyone and everyone in my life, except me, was able to determine my emotional state. I truly was an emotional beggar.

"For the first time I understood the role that I played in the drama of my life. I had begged for my mother's attention, my father's love, my family's respect, my friends' friendship, my colleagues' recognition, my partner's acknowledgement, people's acceptance, Matria's understanding…

"I had begged by being silent, by trying to please, by over-explaining, by complaining, by hating others quietly, by screaming at them loudly, by wanting them to be what they were not, by making my well-being dependent on their actions. I had begged under so many covers that I had even fooled myself. That was a harsh truth to encounter.

"Exhausted and shocked, I walked out of Matria's home and wandered for hours. I could not believe the very behavior I had worked so hard to develop and thought so liberating had kept me captive emotionally. This discovery led to a U-turn in my life."

"What a story, Lamenti. I'm exhausted just from listening. If this is the definition of a beggar, then I wonder if I too have been begging in various forms, not at work, but in my personal life."

Lamenti gave Milan a sympathetic, knowing look: "These memories still take me for a ride. I think our emotions are informing us that we need to break for today. What do you say? Shall we reconvene tomorrow?"

"Interesting, I was thinking let's soldier on, but you're right, it would be better if I come back tomorrow."

"That's the beauty of being an emotional Attentionist—there's no need to soldier on, because we're no longer in the war zone of a Survivalist life."

"You definitely have found your voice, Lamenti."

"Thank you. I have gone from no voice, to an unhealthy Survivalist pseudo-voice, to a healthy Attentionist true voice!"

With these words Lamenti brought the conversation to an end. They both got up and left the colorful living room, feeling their way through the even more colorful—and sometimes uncomfortable—feelings and emotions their conversation had stirred.

6

LAMENTI, AN EMOTIONAL ATTENTIONIST II

Milan left Lamenti's with a hopeful mind and a heavy heart. The unresolved grief over Sky's sudden death many years earlier—a loss he had quietly carried but never truly confronted—now hit him hard. Seated in his air-car, tears began to flow as he wondered—had he chosen the feeling of love, might Sky still be alive? He had so many questions about his emotions, but answers eluded him. Nevertheless, the act of finally shedding tears after such a long time brought a sense of openness and relief.

Milan returned the next day as planned and Lamenti received him with fresh energy. Once again they drank saffron tea. This time, Milan noticed how unusual and delicious it was.

"What *is* this tea, Lamenti? The color and fragrance are most enticing. Plus I feel strangely happy as I sip."

Lamenti smiled knowingly: "It's Persian saffron, a spice that comes from Iran. It's the most precious herb in the world, and one of the most marvelous. It takes three years to crop, and 70,000 flowers to produce a single pound. It has many beneficial properties, but mainly it makes you feel good. Seriously. It was used in the old world as an anti-depressant."

"I believe it," Milan said with an appreciative nod. "No wonder I had such a good time yesterday. By the way, thank you for being in touch with your emotions and suggesting we take a break. Powering through is what I usually do, but this was much better, especially for the kind of conversation we've been having. It also allowed *me* to connect to some of my own old and unfelt emotions." Milan paused, but decided not to elaborate, and turned the conversation back to his primary mission.

"On my drive here and while reviewing our talk and your story, I wondered how many people—on Earth or on Ours—would reach the same conclusions as you? Believing that pretense, silence, complaining, even huffing and puffing make you strong and emotionally free, though you're so fragile that you lose it often, and in many cases, never find it."

"Many people," Lamenti said, "here, and inevitably on planet Ours. But the problem isn't just huffing and puffing or blowing your top. Survivalists also go to the other extreme and shut down emotionally. They disconnect. It's an instinctive form of self-protection—*if I don't feel, I can't hurt.* And over time, the damage builds up. Repressed feelings catch up with you one way or another, through physical symptoms, uncontrollable impulses, or personal crisis."

Milan stared at Lamenti. Was the last comment aimed at him? Did Lamenti somehow sense what he was going through, that he had repressed his pain around the death of Sky, and that his quest to find wisdom for planet Ours was bringing it all up?

A warm and daring tension hovered in the air. Milan lanced it gently: "I get that Survivalism plays out emotionally in different ways. My question now is, what's the healthy version of emotional connection? The one we achieve when we have a true voice, an Attentionist voice, as you called it. And how do we get there?"

"The healthy state is emotional independence," Lamenti replied. "It's the opposite of emotional begging, co-dependence, or repression. And, as with all Attentionism, it centers on choice."

"I like how that sounds, but how does one go from emotional begging to emotional independence and choice?"

Lamenti lit up at the question: "I learned a way. There's a healthy, quiet space in our emotional world, where our feelings and emotions can meet and converse. I call it the Neutral-Room. This place is crucial to emotional independence and health. It's like the Observation-Deck of the mind—Menso told you about that, right?—except we go here to actively witness our emotions in a non-engaged manner, and receive the gifts they have come to give."

"By non-engaged do you mean not caring too much, or at all?"

"No. Non-engaged is not the same as disengaged or not caring. It just means we're not entangled and reactive. We're not engaged with an agenda. We're a neutral but active witness to what's going on inside, able to use our emotions as a prompt to identify and create feelings we'd like to have. The Neutral-Room allows us to do that by receiving and treating our emotions non-emotionally, as information."

"*Emotion as information*," Milan repeated. "Is that what you meant by receiving the gift?

"Yes, exactly. There are two ways we can receive our emotions: emotionally or informationally. The first is when we experience what comes up in us without any mediation, like an infant who is overwhelmed by anger, fear, grief, or joy. There's a purity to that, but it doesn't last. As we grow up, we experience emotions through a thick filter of memories. Emotions we've held on to, with little or no choice, participation, or conscious say. These old, stale, emotions have already made a decision about incoming new ones. That's why we see habitual negative patterns of interaction between people.

"For example, that night I perceived my mother's words through the filter of old emotions, as an attack, so I started attacking her in turn, acting out my library of negative emotions. I was reacting, like a Survivalist, without any real sense of choice. Taking a pause and sitting in the Neutral-Room to center in choice is the antithesis of this.

"Let's imagine I had gone there and received my emotions informationally. The same emotions I felt in reaction to my mom—anger, longing, pain—would have informed me that what I really wanted to feel was love. As an emotionally independent person instead of a desperate begging one, I would have paid attention to love and acted lovingly toward myself, whatever that may have meant to me in that moment. Perhaps going slower, or sitting down and drinking a warm cup of tea, or taking off my shoes and feeling the earth, or so many other small loving things that allow us to go from harsh to gentle.

"With my intention and attention on love, my actions would have created energies in my body of the same quality. At the very least I would have treated myself lovingly, and at the very best I would have treated others lovingly as well, inviting their loving energy, when or if available.

"It's a change of terms between our emotions and ourselves. Their length of employment goes from permanent to temporary, and their job goes from deciding for us, to meeting us in the Neutral-Room and presenting us with information so that we can decide for ourselves how we want to respond. In a sense, our Attentionist self becomes the CEO and our emotions become our helpful employees."

Milan smiled. "As a CEO, I like your analogy. In the last few generations, we as a species seem to have gone from ignoring our emotions and being stoic, to learning to acknowledge them, to giving them all free rein, and now, maybe, to this new way that you're suggesting. Which sounds like the next step in our emotional evolution—be aware, in a neutral state, let them in, and get them to work for you, *in-form* you, and help you arrive at the feelings you really want to have. This seems evolutionary and revolutionary. And it sounds very promising for planet Ours."

"I found it extremely helpful, Milan. Remember: pleasant emotions tell us that we're close to or inside our desired feelings. And unpleasant emotions tell us what feelings we would like to experience that we're not experiencing now. It's a simple informational relationship with our emotions, all of them. Be they pleasant or unpleasant, wanted or unwanted, welcome or unwelcome, they're all at our service, and hence, as you suggest, at the service of all."

bellhops!

Milan took in Lamenti's cheerful face and smiled, but despite his enthusiasm, he had a reservation about what he had just heard.

"Much as I like this approach as a clean engineering model of the emotions, it seems counter-intuitive to experience them this way, as information. Isn't that unnatural, and hard?" he asked.

"Not at all," Lamenti replied. "Let me share a visual with you that might make it easier. I like seeing emotions as old-fashioned bellhops walking around the lobby of my Attentionist Hotel, calling out loud to meet me in the Neutral-Room of the hotel, and give me a piece of information for my wellbeing.

"A bellhop was calling me out that night with my mom, and telling me, Lamenti, you are not feeling loved the way you long to be. And I, instead of concluding that I longed to experience love, was forcefully chasing the bellhop, holding on to them and their message, and demanding that my mother change it for me.

"I could have met and received their information in the Neutral-Room, thanked them and let them go, and gone about gifting myself with that which I was begging my mother for. I didn't truly need my mother's intervention, though it would of course been delightful to have. The problem, Matria says, is what we don't offer ourselves, we wish, hope, expect, and even demand from others.

"The irony is it's much easier to get what we want when we know what it is and begin to give it to ourselves. Which leads me to another one of Matria's principles—do you have your pencil ready?—things work out more easily and quickly when we go from energy to matter instead of the other way around."

"You lost me there, Lamenti. Energy to matter, what's that got to do with emotions?"

"Let me explain. When we wait for something external to change in order to feel a certain way, that's matter to energy. We want matter—something concrete happening in the outside world—to bring about an energy, a feeling of well-being in us. The famous 'I'll feel great *when....*' On the other hand, when we choose a feeling and allow ourselves to act accordingly, then we're going from energy to matter. Our energy of choice to our matter of action, and our desired result.

"Have you ever experienced yourself in a state of flow, when things happen smoothly? Or in an un-flow state, when the smallest tasks are cumbersome? That's the difference between energy to matter and matter to energy. Flow, which means you're in the desired state of energy, brings about desired experiences easily and effortlessly. Of course, energy and matter are interdependent. But energy is primary in non-Survivalist circumstances, such as getting things done, overcoming challenges, and best of all, feeling good!"

"Lamenti, I'm afraid this kind of emotional metaphysics is a little beyond me right now, but I'll try to remember it next time I'm in a state of un-flow! It sounds like what you're saying though about energy and matter is related to emotional independence, and choice. Is that right?"

"Very much so, Milan. Choosing to change our energy first—our inner state—and letting the rest follow. Remember the triangle of genes, history, and choice? Choice is at the top. That's the key. Sovereignty is the result of activating choice in the Triangle-of-Self.

"Choice is a decision and inner energy, which, when tapped, leads to outer actions. As we free ourselves from our taught and practiced Survivalist mentality, we see our dance with the world and the people in it as an exciting opportunity to create and define ourselves. It is in these interactions that we clarify our chosen dance, select the music accordingly, and leave others to find their own."

"Are you saying we shouldn't—or don't—have a say in how others dance, to use your metaphor?" Milan asked.

"I'm saying the best way to influence others, if and when they are ready, is by dancing to our own music of wellbeing and feeling good. Our energy—the frequency we create as we dance—influences their matter. On the other hand, demanding, forcing, or any other form of begging, does not and has not changed others in a sustainable way. It's not supposed to. It would compromise their freedom of choice if it did."

Milan quickly objected: "Wait a minute—helping others to change for better and grow compromises their freedom of choice?"

"If they don't wish or are not ready to change and grow, absolutely!"

"That's a little hard for me to digest. I often push people to change for better."

"Remember, Matria's initial story started because the gift of choice and free will was honored by the Big-Everything. We can and eventually will all go back to being Little-Everythings, because that is where we belong, but only when we choose to do so. We got here by choice and we can only get out of here by choice."

"I hear what you're saying but I need time to fathom this one, Lamenti. As I say, I have always pushed people, and many have enjoyed and benefited from it."

"Then those many people were willing to move forward, which is why they enjoyed it. While those who weren't willing, did not. Simple!"

electro-magnetic?

Milan and Lamenti sat pleasantly without a word. Their conversation had left a soft hum in their ears and minds. Milan looked at his new friend admiringly.

"I have to say, Lamenti, you've answered my questions without pressuring me in any way to become an Attentionist or adopt your views. The same with Sukseso and Menso. I'm really impressed by that, and I know I've had many questions, and haven't agreed with you in all points. Speaking of which, I have one more! Menso said you were the best person to ask about the electro-magnetic nature of thoughts and emotions. Can you explain that to me before I leave?"

Lamenti's eyes brightened and their arms once again began to dance, sleeves flowing like streamers. As they settled, they looked at Milan and dove in: "You've probably heard that thoughts are electric and emotions magnetic. One carries force and the other attraction. Does this remind you of anything?"

"No, I'm not sure what you mean?"

"For example, masculine energy and feminine energy?"

"Now that you mention it, yes. But I'm surprised—are you saying thoughts are masculine and emotions are feminine? That's so retro."

"Not *literally,* but energetically speaking they feel like they behave that way. Let me unfold this further.

"In a Survivalist state, thought and emotion, the mind and heart are separate. But in a non-Survivalist state they are a unified field, two aspects of one. They're partners, meaning part of each other, not rivals. In fact, more accurately they should be called heart/mind, and many old cultures do just that; they use heart and mind interchangeably as a single word to refer to both.

"With Attentionism, heart and mind have an opportunity to re-unite. The feminine aspect of heart/mind conceives the seed of an idea—not by thinking, but through feeling, sensing, and deep resonance. It embraces the seed magnetically, like a silent yes to something not yet visible.

"The masculine aspect of heart/mind, the mind, perceives what the heart has conceived. It recognizes the essence, gives it thought-form, and powers a pathway for its expression. The full being—heart, mind, and body—then receives the experience that this unity brings into the world.

"In other words: the heart conceives, the mind perceives, and the whole self receives. That's how the invisible becomes visible— through the union of heart-mind, masculine-feminine, and the electro-magnetic field. Together, without interference, they bring ideas into existence in a natural, coherent, interdependent process."

"Wow! That's a mouthful, Lamenti! I *think* I follow. Are you saying that when heart and mind are united and interdependent, the heart's decision and mind's implementation result in creativity and wellbeing?"

"Exactly. We all know this, the feeling we have when we follow our passion and become invincible. Our heart, in unity with the mind, has created a passionate idea, and our mind, in wholeness with the heart, does whatever is necessary to fulfill that passion and materialize it. Together, heart and mind make the impossible possible, and the possible magical. Plus, the masculine and feminine energies that we all have are balanced. You must have experienced this yourself at times, to be where you are, no?"

"I have, but not knowingly and not as often as I would have liked," Milan replied. "Also, without having the language for it. Especially the masculine-feminine part. As a man I still find it somewhat awkward to think in those terms."

"Ah yes, but it's so liberating, and empowering. Because it's energetically true. We are not divided beings, all masculine *or* feminine, heart *or* mind. We are unified wholes. And together, within and without, we can get things done.

"Plus, feminine-masculine integration is a prime practice and precedent for oneness while living in the realm of duality and polarity. Imagine holding contrast without contradiction, diversity without adversity. In the context of Matria's story, imagine being Little-Everythings living in the Something's land, enjoying our physical experiences without the suffering produced by our separation from the Source, self, and other beings."

The two sat silently again, absorbing their exchange. Eventually the silence generated a new question:

"Let me ask you something personal, Lamenti—do you consider your old self a Survivalist?"

"Absolutely, one can be a Survivalist with different accents; physical, mental, emotional, even spiritual."

"Oh, spiritual? Tell me more about spiritual Survivalism. That's a new concept I'd like to understand."

"Alas, I am not the best person to help you with that. You need to talk to Devota about their experience. It's a powerful story that will rock your worlds, Earth or Ours. I'd love to share more, but please excuse me. I have to go and get ready for my Crying Party now."

"Your *what* party," Milan asked, with a double-take that made Lamenti laugh.

"You heard me right. My Crying Party. In my journey of becoming an Attentionist, I realized that sometimes we need to do more than vent with words or find our way to the Neutral-Room and connect to our desired feelings. That's not always enough."

"But I thought your journey was about choosing happy, positive, feelings," Milan protested, visibly uncomfortable with the idea of succumbing to tears. "Surely that means choosing *not* to wallow in pain."

Lamenti smiled: "Visiting is not the same as wallowing, my friend. Remember the tourist visa, the limited, purposeful trips to the past? That's how we reconnect with our tears. And believe me, I *had* to. Growing up in my family there was no room for crying—even though I felt emotionally and physically relieved whenever I broke the rules and did.

"As an Attentionist, I began to think about our widespread cultural suppression of tears, and I wondered: When people say, "Please don't cry," is that really about comforting the crier—or protecting themselves from discomfort? Crying has a bad reputation, but if our intelligent bodies have given us this natural function to express, connect, release, and reset... why not use it?"

"This is too much," Milan said, vexed, perplexed, and, truth be told, more than a little threatened. One part of him wanted to explore his own unshed tears, which were signaling a dangerous inclination to break through. A stronger part was terrified of doing so."

"Hear me out, Milan," Lamenti continued. "At the start of every equinox and solstice, I host a Crying Party—a safe, supportive gathering where guests come together by choice with the intention of clearing their history and adjusting the volume on their genes so they can reclaim their emotional independence.

"We sit in a circle. Each person shares a brief story about an overstayed emotion, then identifies the message it carries—the 'bellhop announcement.' We reflect on any action we've taken or want to take based on that message. And in the process, if tears come, we welcome them.

"Most of us feel a sense of release, connection, and unexpected joy when we cry. The group holds space—no advice, no fixing, no judgment—just the human gift of being vulnerable and seen. You can't imagine how good that usually feels.

"And then we end the party with music, mindful moving, and breaking healthy breads together. Crying somehow unites us with our Little-Everything-*ness*. It shifts our view—from the Survivalist mindset that sees crying as weak or inappropriate, to the Attentionist perspective, which honors crying as a human experience and a tool for expression, and expansion.

"We now have a waiting list for upcoming parties, and I'm training facilitators around the globe. You're welcome to join us when and if you choose. Despite what we've been told by institutions and social norms, crying can be a joyful and healthy experience."

With these words, Lamenti discreetly excused themself, pretending they had not noticed the wetness in Milan's eyes.

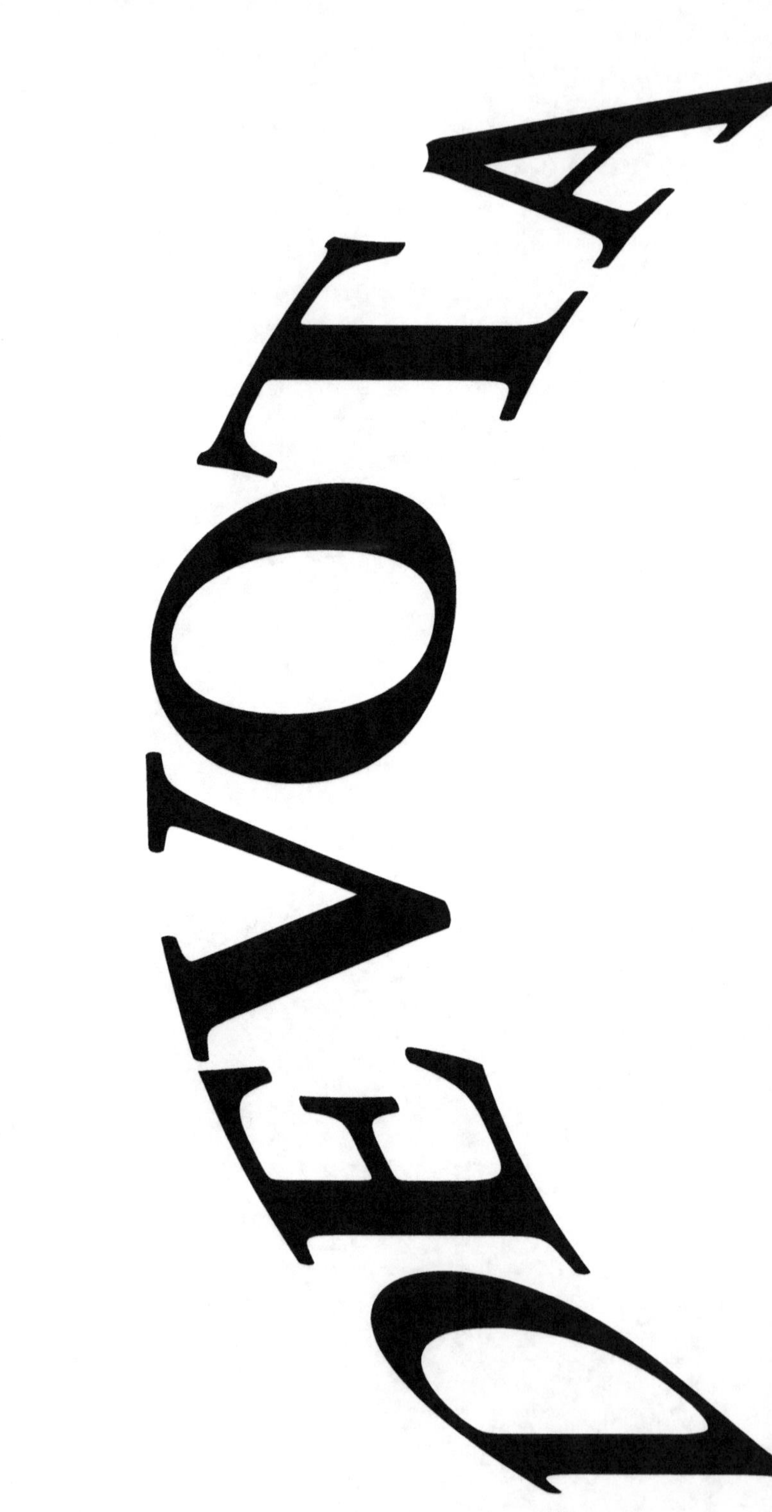

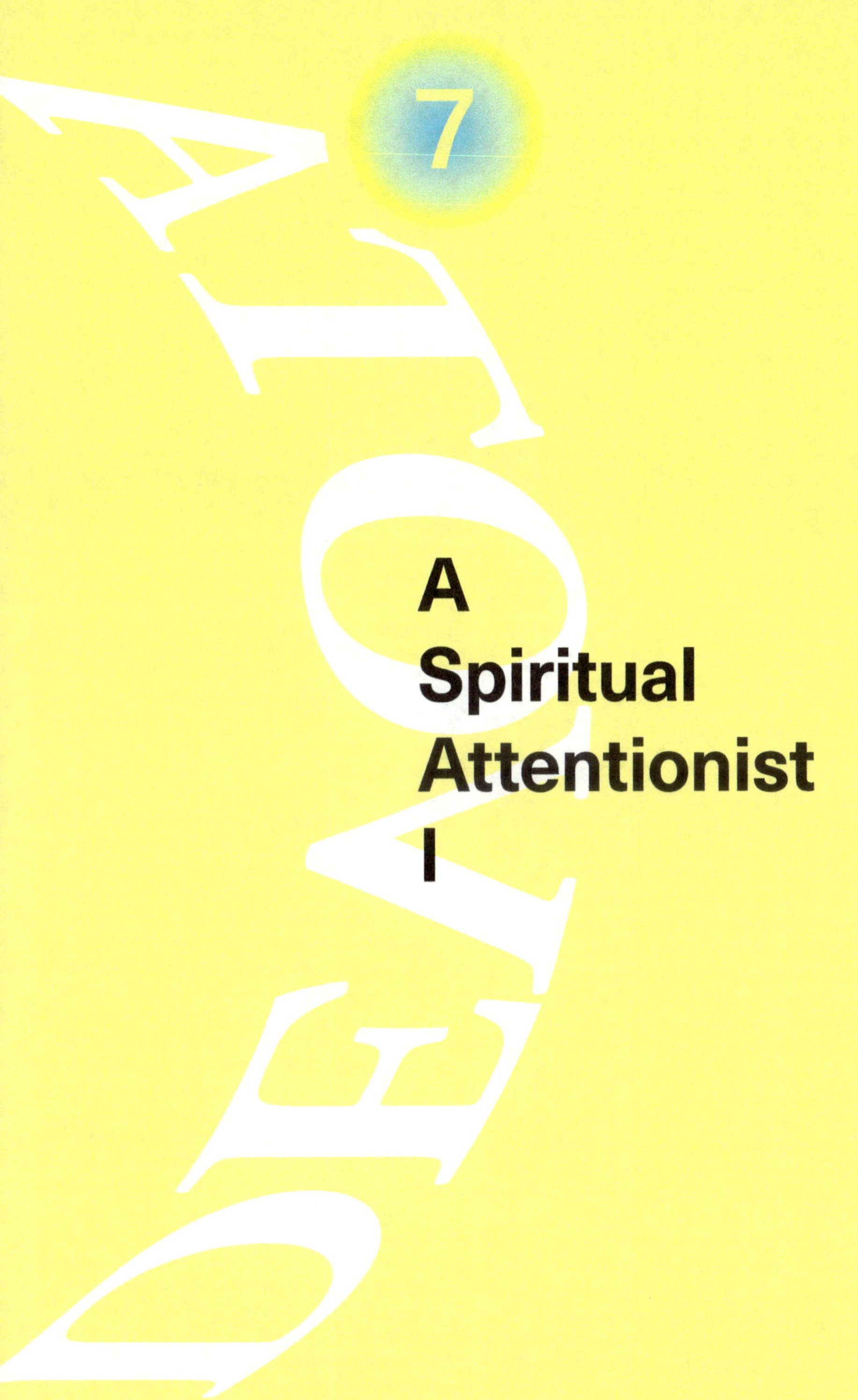
7
A
Spiritual
Attentionist
I

Milan left Lamenti's bright and cheerful home, surprised by a stirring in his heart, an opening really, that he hadn't felt in a long time. He reviewed the many insights Lamenti had shared about the world of emotions: feelings vs. emotions; begging vs. independence; venting vs. complaining; receiving emotions informationally; hanging out in the Neutral-Room; feminine and masculine energies; and most importantly, the triangle of choice + genes + history.

Then too, there was the "Crying Party," and the question of Milan's own unexpressed emotions and withheld tears. He decided to take the next day off to get better acquainted with his neglected and rejected emotional life.

But after a good night's sleep, Milan's old confidence came back and he wondered if he really needed to dig deep inside himself after all. He sat in the imaginary Neutral-Room Lamenti told him about, and examined where in life he did not live with choice. In much of his life, he couldn't find any real evidence of choicelessness. He took pride in his ability to do what he wanted to do and not be a victim of social or family norms. True, he had some disturbing blind spots, and there were certain feelings and memories that he found impossible to face. But he figured this was normal, inevitable in fact, over the course of a full life. And he wasn't aware of any bellhops chasing him, at least not at the moment. He concluded that Lamenti's journey might be useful for others, but not for him. Nevertheless, he remained inquisitive about his emotions, and his relationship to them.

That afternoon, Kuriozi, who rarely saw her dad at home during the day, asked if he would attend a performance at a school fundraising event in which she was playing a role she was excited about: an alien girl discovering Earth's strange ways. Milan brushed the invitation off, saying he was too busy with work that day. Kuriozi asked him about the nature of his busyness, but Milan got agitated and repeated, "I just can't, I have work to do."

Kuriozi didn't let it go as she really wanted her dad to be there and watch her perform for a good cause, so she dug deeper: "What is your *busy-ness* about, dad, and why can't it be changed?"

Milan, perturbed by Kuriozi's insistence, said loudly: "My father never attended my school performances or events. He focused on his work and that didn't stop me from learning, did it?!"

Kuriozi, stunned by her father's unusual dictatorial tone, said: "But that's not a reasonable answer, Dad. I need to know why so I can understand your world better, or convince you to come to my school so that you can better understand mine." Lowering her voice, she added: "Really Dad, with all of your innovative ideas and inventions, you just do what your dad did without question or reason? That's so Attentionist of you!" And she left the room.

A cold smile appeared on Milan's face as he recalled his smug contemplation of the morning. He felt tight, hot, and agitated. He remembered Lamenti's teachings and asked himself: *What just happened? What are my emotions, and what are they trying to tell me about my harsh words and the feelings that I want? Can parenting perhaps be where I have not activated my choices, emotionally, and am stuck between my genes and history? If so, where else do I have blind spots and unknowingly act out like a Survivalist?*

Milan sat in his empty room, feeling strangely bittersweet. It was thrilling to become aware of his emotions—shame, sadness, dismay—but not so thrilling to think he might be parenting Kuriozi reactively, in survival mode.

Later that night, Milan went to Kuriozi's room and asked her about her school event and her role in the play, and he told her about his commitment that Friday. He wanted to feel connected with Kuriozi, and his emotions informed him he was on the wrong road, far away from connection. The final decision? Well, Milan arranged to work at a private office in Kuriozi's school that day, which allowed him to have a virtual meeting and attend her performance.

In the days that followed, Milan felt good about his fresh relationship with his emotions—and Kuriozi—and looked forward to connecting with Devota and traveling to the unknown land of spirituality.

does truth matter?

As un-religious as Milan was, he was deeply intrigued by how a spiritual Attentionist might differ from the religious people he knew. With this curiosity, he reached out to Devota and arranged a meeting.

Devota greeted Milan with a calm and generous smile, but limited words. Milan felt a bit uncomfortable with the long pauses that they offered him, so instead of giving them the whole spiel about why he was there, he simply asked Devota if they knew anything about his project, to which they answered, yes, enough to proceed with the meeting.

Devota's home was minimalistic and simple, yet warm and welcoming. Every item in the living room had a function and a reason for being there. Comfortable seating with orange cushions covered three sides of the room. A long low coffee table held paper and pen, two lamps, two tall glasses, and a bottle of water with mint and lemon. There was no decoration or ornamentation, but glass walls merged the room with trees and shrubberies and flowers outside.

The space felt peaceful and Devota felt like a content, wise, and kind person. Milan had no idea what to expect from this meeting. So he asked them to start wherever they wanted. They took their time and then began with a calm and unrushed tone.

"I come from a religious family and background and was an active member of my religious community as an adult. I strongly believed in what my religion offered, and in my mind, I served my faith community very well by being a devoted volunteer and attending religious events and ceremonies. Until one day, around one of our special holidays, when we decided to invite representatives of other religious groups to participate in a panel discussion on the topic of 'truth matters.'

"We saw ourselves as open-minded and we thought this kind of event and discussion would be a great way of being inclusive while expanding our reach to potential community members. Someone on the organizing committee suggested that we invite Matria, a teacher who did not represent any isms, but was well-versed in the world of spirituality and well-liked by the youth of our community. It sounded like a great, progressive idea to have a woman not from the mainstream, and representing no particular religion, on the panel. Plus, we wanted to attract younger people. Matria was invited, and she agreed to come."

"I'd like to have been there for that panel," Milan said warmly. "Matria must have talked about Attentionism, right, and Little-Everythings?"

"No, in fact she did not say a word during our very lively panel discussions. Not a word."

"That's strange, why?"

Devota smiled: "You see, our event was a success. Hundreds of people showed up, we ran out of seats, and people were standing for hours to listen to our discussions. As a moderator of the event, I assumed Matria was experiencing stage fright and that's why she was not speaking. I saw her as a simple teacher who wasn't used to strong discussions with well-known experts like our panelists, or a large audience such as ours.

"So, before we ended the event, for the sake of decorum and respect, I asked her if she had anything to add. Matria said she had been listening deeply to us as we all spoke about the truth from our own religious perspectives, and she would like to ask all panelists, as well as the audience, one question."

Milan was very curious, indeed: "What was her question?"

"She asked all nine panelists if they ever found themselves standing at a fork where, to their right was the truth, and to their left was their own religion's reality on a subject, which way would they choose? She then turned to our audience, and said this question is also for all of you.

"A very uncomfortable silence took over the stage and the entire hall. I could hear the hearts of panelists beating and their tongues struggling in their dry mouths. Many reached for their drinks. A few started coughing nervously. One looked petrified. One pretended to be taking notes. And I, I felt nervous to my core. To save us all from this awkward discomfort and insight-provoking question, I broke the silence and declared that I would go with the truth, of course, no doubt.

"Many panelists followed my path of good and safe PR and said the same thing, more or less. None of us sounded convincing, but all of us felt relieved after responding to Matria's question. I thanked the panelists and wrapped up the discussion hastily. Music and refreshments followed and took the sting out of a really difficult ending that was felt by all, but mentioned by none."

truth vs. reality

"I'm so interested to find out more, but before you go on can you tell me what the difference is between the reality of something and the truth of it?" Milan asked.

"I see you pay attention to words. The truth of any matter is One, no matter who sees/accepts/seeks it, and who does not. Reality is our version of the truth. It may or may not be the truth, or the whole truth, but it is what we believe to be true. So there is the truth and then there is our understanding of it, which becomes our reality.

"It's like the famous Rumi story of the elephant that was brought to Persia for the first time and kept in a dark room. People who were curious about the elephant went into the room and each touched it from the place they were standing. The one touching his ears declared that an elephant is like a large fan. The one touching his leg declared that an elephant is like a column. The one touching his trunk declared that an elephant is like a rain gutter.

"The room was dark and their views were limited, and they each could only see, touch and report on one part of what a whole, true elephant was like. Their belief about an elephant was limited to their access to the partial truth, hence the discrepancy and incompleteness of their declarations. Matria says there is one truth, and as many realities as there are people in the world."

Milan mulled Devota's analogy. "In this case there would be one truth and as many realities as there were panelists on the panel."

"As many realities as there were people in the room," Devota corrected.

"What happened after the event?"

"Organizers declared it a success, but I went home feeling

confused and disturbed. Deep down I knew I may not have told the truth when I answered Matria's question about the truth. This knowing started to torment me, as truth-telling and truth-seeking was a huge part of my journey. My whole argument with non-religious people was based on the fact that I believed and practiced the truth.

"I could not get her question out of my awareness. What if we don't hold the truth or at least the whole truth? What if the structure we have built to protect the truth is separating us from the truth? I would wake up in the middle of the night sweating, doubting and unsettled. I would imitate Matria's voice, ask myself the question, and then answer it, but without feeling convinced or satisfied. I began neglecting my responsibilities both at home and at work. I stopped volunteering at my place of worship. I felt unresolved, jumpy, and reactive for no particular reason."

"It's remarkable how a single question can rattle a person's world," Milan observed.

"Well, The power of questioning is profound, especially the right question. It's not answers that we're short of in life, it is true and powerful questions that are rare. Anyway, it became excruciating to dwell on this question again and again. Finally I decided to do something unusual. I took some time off from everything, something I had not done for decades, as I was either working for a living or volunteering for the dying."

"Volunteering for dying?"

"Yes, I would pray and assist dying people in my faith community to leave their body peacefully, and that was my main volunteer work."

"What an unusual offering. Did taking time off from everything help?"

"No, it made it worse. Now I had time to torture myself full-time. But the pause gifted me with a decision—I resolved to go and meet Matria in person, in private, and unfold what needed to be unfolded."

Devota went quiet as they remembered, and a gentle smile appeared on their face when they continued: "Matria was not surprised to see me at all, and the first thing she asked when I arrived at her home was—'have you come to talk about your answer?' I told her I was not truthful about the answer I had given her on that day, but I wanted to do whatever it took to keep my answer, and mean it honestly and truthfully."

"I'm not sure I follow," Milan said.

"Basically, I was telling Matria that I wanted to arrive at a place and a consciousness that would allow me to choose the truth over my own practiced beliefs, reality, religion, and community, if and when needed."

"Well, that's the ultimate courage, isn't it," Milan observed. "That must've been huge for you."

"Huge may not do justice to the turbulence I was feeling. You see, my entire story, my identity, and my worth had all been built around my religion and my religious community. It defined who I thought I was, and how I saw my life philosophically, politically, and practically. I always introduced myself as a person of faith, my particular faith, of course. I wanted to be ready to turn my back on all of that for the love of the truth. That is as huge as it could get for me!"

"As much as I don't know a lot about your world, Devota, I can feel the importance and intensity of your quest. What did Matria say?"

"Matria said nothing in the beginning. She left it up to me. She didn't want to come between me and my freedom of choice.

I asked her to help me get out of the tormented state I was in. She said I was in labor, giving birth to the true me, and when the time came, when I was ready, she would midwife me through it. But, she emphasized, she could not make it happen on my behalf. The decision had to come from me, and only from me."

Milan was never interested in religion, but he found Devota's story riveting: *"And?"*

"I pondered and wandered for a few days, and eventually I called Matria and told her I'm ready to explore the birth of the true me. I extended my leave and started studying with Matria. I shared many puzzling questions that suddenly surfaced in my awareness with her, and we walked through them together for hours, days, and weeks."

spiritual survivalists

"Then something interesting happened," Devota continued. "As I accessed a more profound understanding of things related to my soul, the spirit, and my relationship with the Source—or Big-Everything as Matria called it—I got really excited and na-ively enthused. I contacted my fellow panelists, wondering if they too were going through a truth-seeking journey like mine. I arranged to meet with them individually to compare notes, and at the very least give them the benefit of my difficult but exciting path."

"I love your enthusiasm and I can relate to it. How did it work out?" Milan asked.

"I invited them to join me, but no one showed any interest in exploring things beyond their set beliefs. Some came politely, listened and left. Some never showed up. Some exchanged words with me in a politically correct fashion, but weren't motivated in truth-seeking beyond what they had already done."

Milan looked at Devota sympathetically: "Tell me, how did it feel when your passion for truth was not well-received by others? I ask because I've had similar experiences as an innovator, where people want to maintain the status quo and avoid delving into something different and unsettling."

"I felt heart-broken and disappointed by their responses, but excited and hopeful for the expansion of my own spiritual world. I figured I'd have a much better chance if I took my invitation to my community, people who I knew and who knew me in a deeper sense and for a much longer time. And so I did."

"I assume your community showed a deeper interest in the truth?" Milan conjectured.

"Incorrect assumption. In fact, they reacted harshly and unfairly, way worse than my fellow panelists. They implied that I was undermining my roots, betraying and harming my community, and they started attacking Matria for turning me against them. I could not believe that none of them were interested in the discussion about the truth, but deeply interested in protecting the institution to which they belonged. The very institution and individuals claiming to represent the truth, had no interest in investigating it beyond their un-examined, or partially-examined beliefs."

"How do you know their beliefs were un-examined or partially-examined?"

"Because if they had fully examined them, they would have been thrilled to help me do the same. They did not want to even consider that there might be an aspect of the truth that they had not paid full attention to, let alone discuss the nature of it. I was shocked and devastated."

"What a journey, Devota. What did Matria say about all this?"

"Matria was not surprised at all. She said it makes complete sense since spiritual Survivalists believe and live with limited and fear-based choices. I had never heard that term being used in this context before. I asked her to elaborate, and it was then that she told me all about Survivalists, Attentionists, and Eternalists.

"Through a long process of discussion, examination and observation, I understood what living in survival mode had done to humanity in general, and to me and my religious community in particular. It became clear how every healthy intention can turn into its opposite when we live with fear at the root. Spirituality can turn into dense political-ism. Love can turn into control. Unity can turn into sameness. Connection with the Source can turn into a transactional exchange of prayer and expectation. Wanting liberation for others can turn into unhealthy over-protection. Community can turn into lack of diversity and freedom. I realized I needed to get out of that world before I got even more contaminated by the spiritual Survivalist virus."

Devota shuddered as they recalled their narrow escape.

"Did you share your findings with your community and fellow panelists before leaving them?" Milan asked.

"I tried many times. I wanted to press the issue and tell them how they had gone about something as healthy as truth-seeking with an unhealthy energy of fear. I reached out again and again but the more I tried the more I experienced their lack of interest and openness to fresh discussions and truth-seeking exploration.

"When I shared this with Matria she said I didn't have the ability or right to change anyone's journey, unless and until they wanted to do so first. She believed having an agenda for others, even a healthy agenda, would only result in the delay of their journey to truth. There was no need and no use in insisting and sharing.

"I also learned that most of the time it is not information that Survivalists are missing, it's the level of consciousness and density of fear-based realities that don't allow them to find their way. And in that case, no information or evidence can help change their mind. I freed myself from convincing, converting, or even conversing about the subject. I allocated most of my energy to increasing my own spiritual AQ and working through my own spiritual Survivalist conditioning." As part of that process, I eventually left the community I had devoted myself to for more than thirty years.

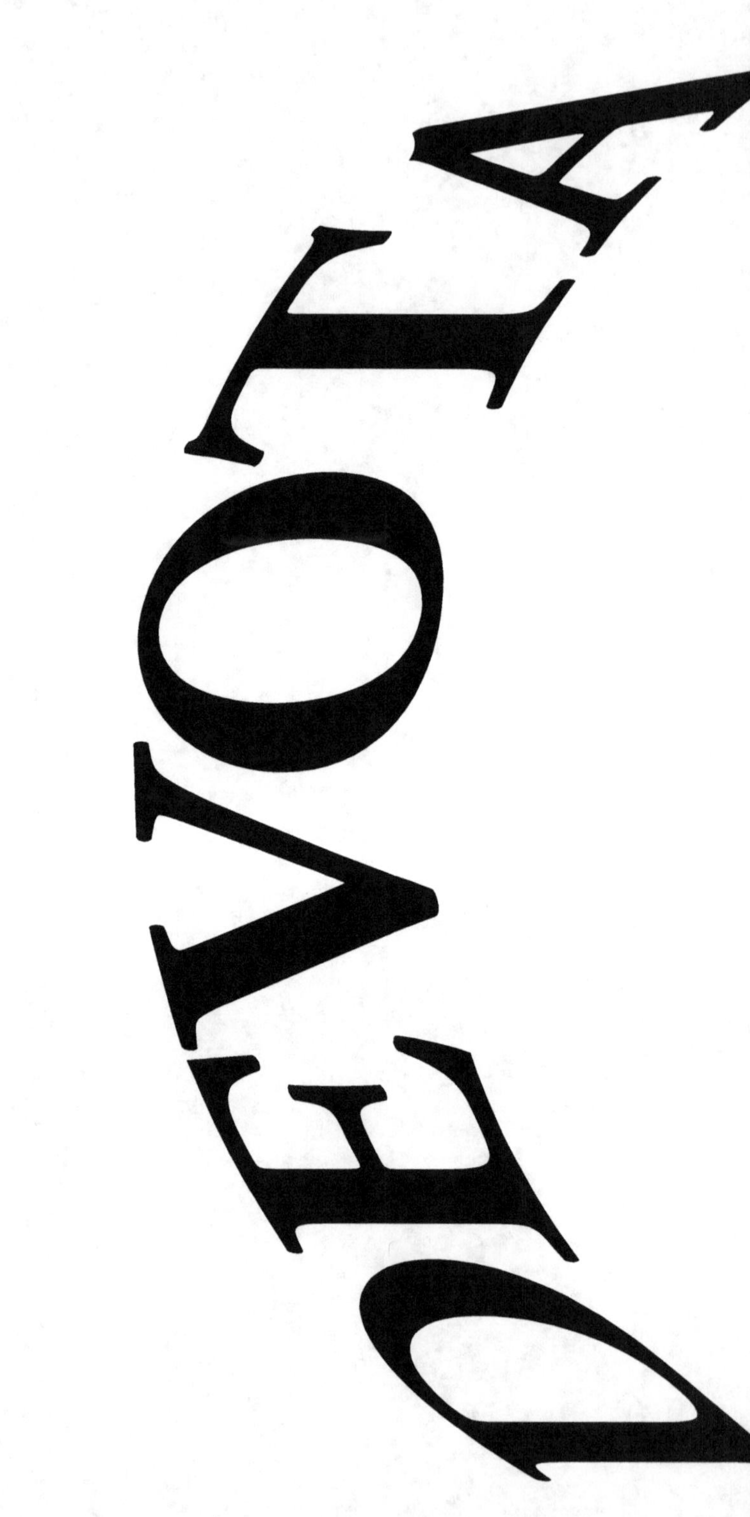

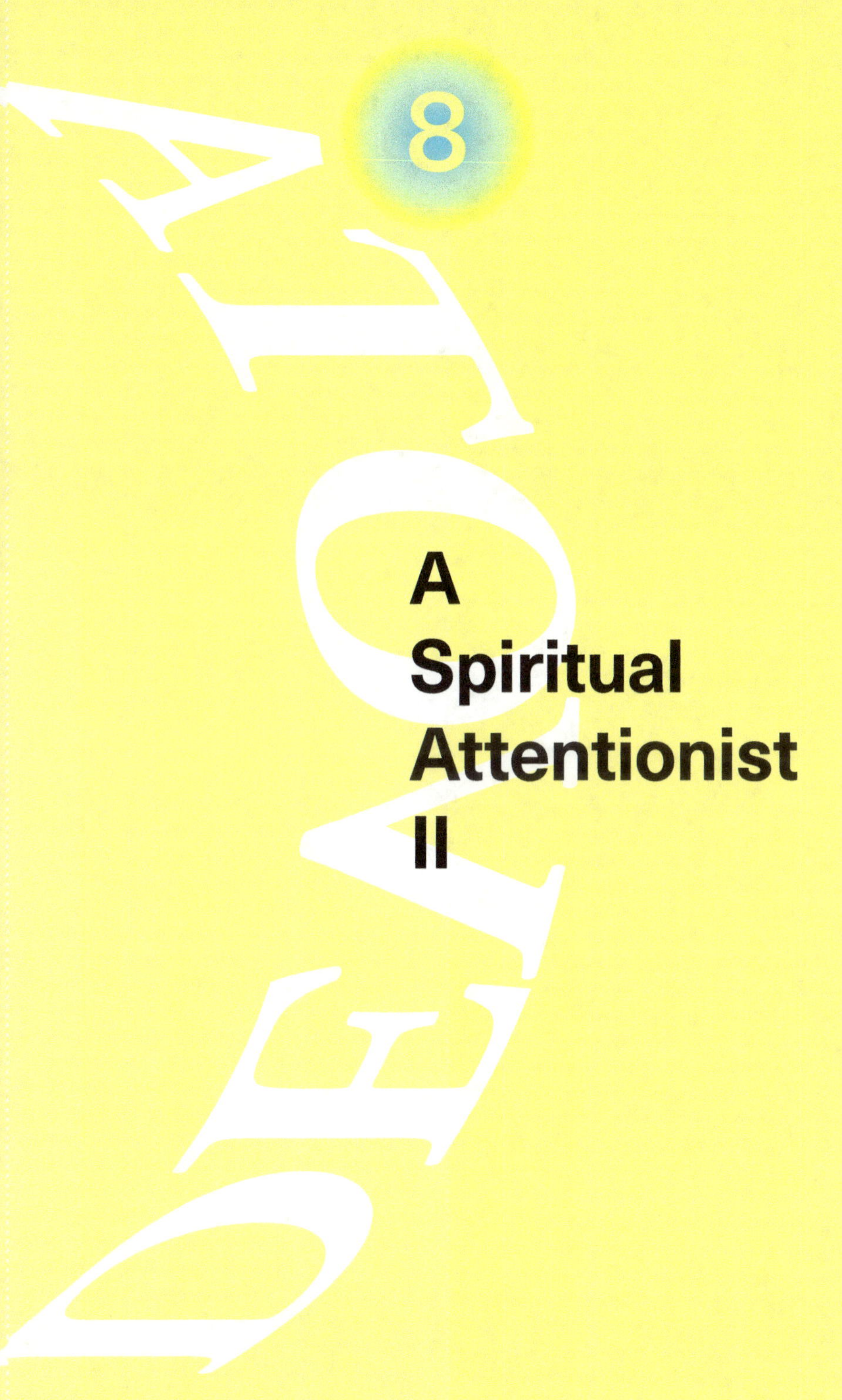
ATOM
8
A
Spiritual
Attentionist
II

Devota and Milan sat in silence for a while. The silence just happened, and Milan, to his surprise, was not uncomfortable with it. To the contrary, he loved the okay-ness of not having to keep the conversation going and think about what to ask next. Devota closed their eyes and started to breathe deeply and slowly. This gave Milan an opportunity to try the same. He stayed in this state until he heard Devota drinking water. Milan opened his eyes, feeling restored and refreshed. A question surfaced naturally about something Devota had touched on earlier.

"Devota, you spoke before about truth and reality. What's the difference between the two in the context of religion?"

"Oh, it's very similar. Spirituality is truth, and religiosity is 'reality.' Religions were supposed to be a door to the truth, but somehow along the way, truth got muddied with the realities of those involved. Meaning those particular religions, the importance and superiority of their followers, and their power over others mattered more than the message they were carrying. This happens in Survivalism. The way becomes the destination. The messenger becomes the message. And the name and fame become the mission."

"Are you saying religions carry their own reality and partial truth?" Milan queried.

"I have no true knowing of all religions to answer this question," Devota modestly replied. "I do know that in general, truth-based messages have gone through the hands of human translation and the minds of human interpretation. That alone is likely to turn any truth into reality, and spirituality into religiosity."

"What a humbling assertion. If that's the case, how does one distinguish between a spiritual person and a religious person?"

"A spiritual or conscious person—by which I mean someone who's aware of being a Little-Everything living in the Somethings' land—is in pursuit of finding the truth and connecting with the Source through the truth, always. A religious person already has a set belief that their religion is the truth, with or without deep examination, and is in pursuit of finding evidence to defend it, prove it, or promote it."

Milan cocked his head to the side: "So you think that a religious person can't be spiritual or conscious?"

"Not at all. In fact, a spiritual person can have a religion, and some do. I am merely sharing my experience about spiritual Survivalists. A spiritual person who practices a religion does so with a deeper knowing that this is not the only way to the truth, it just happens to be their way. They walk that particular religion's path, but their allegiance stays to the truth. It's like we're all going to the airport, and we take different roads because of where our individual homes are located. Then we start arguing with each other as to how the road we're taking is the only way or the most preferred way. What we're missing is that the road we're taking is not the purpose of our journey—arriving at the airport is."

soul vs. spirit

"Thank you, Devota, what a good analogy. I wonder if you can help me with another question: what's the difference between soul and Spirit? I noticed that you distinguish between the two?"

"Milan, you may not be religious, but you sure are curious about spirituality. The simplest way to answer your question is to use Matria's story: Spirit is the soul and the energy of the Big-Everything and our soul is a part of that energy that is animating our individual bodies. In other words, Spirit is the soul of the Source, and your soul is a portion of that which runs in you."

"So my soul is a portion of Spirit?"

"Correct. And what determines your spiritual journey is how connected you are to your own soul, and how connected your soul is to the Spirit. In other words, how self-connected and Source-connected you are."

Milan nodded admiringly. "Devota, that's the simplest explanation of soul and Spirit I have ever heard."

Devota returned the nod: "Simplicity is a good indicator of not being dense. Soul and Source are simple, and indivisible. Unfortunately, in our fear state, we have humanized the Source, the Prime Creator, the Big-Everything, if you like. Just listen to some religious sermons about how vindictive the Source can be, and you'll see what I mean. In Attentionism, we realize we have more and bigger options for understanding the Source."

"Which one have you chosen?" Milan asked.

"I have chosen to see myself Source-like instead of seeing the Source human-like. Of course, that is if we believe that Source even exists."

"And what if we don't?"

"That is also a choice that needs to be respected."

"So if you meet an atheist, you wouldn't try to tell them about Big-Everything and the rest of your learnings?"

"Only if they ask and tell me they're interested in hearing my version of the truth."

"Oh, so your truth is also a reality."

Devota smiled like one who had made mistakes in this regard that they were determined to never repeat again. "Absolutely. That's why I keep exploring it with the intention of taking my partial reality to wholeness and as close as possible to the truth. I may be thinking

I'm seeing a larger portion of the elephant, but I know my view is still limited, and there is much more to unfold. Our collective savings account at the Cosmic Bank of Wisdom, as Menso puts it, is growing in value as elevated beings unfold. Remember, Matria's story of creation started with the Big-Everything wanting to unfold itself. The more I see, the more there is to see. Simple!"

Milan laughed: "Not for everyone, Devota. I honestly thought you would say that your reality is the truth."

"And I *would* have said that as a religious Survivalist, before becoming a spiritual Attentionist."

is God transactional?

"Okay, let me ask you another question," Milan pursued. "Earlier you alluded to a transactional relationship vs. a relational relationship with the Source. Can you tell me more about that?"

"Yes of course. That is an important point. In Survivalism we're separated and deep down we see ourselves less than, not enough, even bad. We still remember what feeling good feels like though, from the time of unity. From that memory, and to pursue that good feeling, we do interesting things, like worshiping the Source in fear, begging for outcomes, making deals in the hope of feeling good and getting what we want. When that doesn't work we go to threatening, sulking, separating from the Source, like an unhealthy relationship gone wrong.

"Once we feel connected, one with, part of the Source, once our soul is connected to the Spirit of the Source, love takes the place of fear, and deep relationship removes any transactional deals we may have had. We don't need to transact with something we're part of; we simply connect with it, and we're right there where we want to be, feeling the feelings, and being in the state that we desperately chased outwardly throughout our lives."

"I feel shivers running through my body as I listen to your words, Devota. What is it that I am feeling?"

"I have no idea, Milan. You need to explore the electricity that is running through your body which you call shivers, on your own. Trust that you know and you don't need to ask me or anyone else."

Milan took his time and sat in silence. He was experiencing things that were unfamiliar to him. *Could this be the* Darlings *helping me because I have chosen to explore the truth, he wondered?* Milan marveled that he was having these conversations and feelings in relation to his quest, which he assumed was most of all a scientific and technological challenge. After a long pause, he turned to Devota, who seemed to be in playful place: "Where are you in your own journey now?"

Devota lit up at the question: "I now am happily playing in the playground of spiritual Attentionism, with the excitement, enthusiasm and joy of eventually becoming an Eternalist!"

the eternalist

Milan was quick to follow-up. "This is the second time you've you've used the word Eternalist. Matria also mentioned it briefly. What does that mean? Is it someone who lives forever?"

Devota laughed quietly: "Sort of. We all exist forever, in different forms, or no physical form at all, but as pure energy. When you exist, you cannot not exist. To answer your question, an Eternalist is a person who remembers who they truly are. They have physicality, of course, but they live from the inside out, so to speak. They pay more attention to their energetic well-being, their soul-Source, and allow that to gift them with physical, mental, and emotional health. They have a knowing about the bigger story of life—a larger portion of the truth. They live mainly in abundance. They mostly think with their Whole-Mind and allow their integrated feminine/masculine energies and deeper feelings of goodness to guide them when working with emotions. Where Survivalists have limited their choices to survival, and Attentionists are exploring their vast variety of choices, Eternalists have already made the fundamental choice for their life to be about unity, creation, and joy.

"We come to this world as Little-Everythings, naturally united with Big-Everything and literally every thing and every being. Then we unlearn that and learn to become Somethings. But we have a choice of completing the cycle of this physical life by remembering and going back to being Little-Everythings, as Eternalists, this time not by nature, but by choice.

"We can choose to either stay disconnected in fear, and leave our body kicking and screaming, or, to choose unity and leave our physical-ness happily, excited to explore what comes. Because in this state we know existence has no end. Again, the conservation of energy assures us of that.

"In short," Devota summed up, "in the Survivalist state our choices are limited to survival. In the Attentionist state our choices are vast. In the Eternalist state there is the fundamental choice of remembering that we're Little-Everythings, part of Big-Everything. All smaller choices are easy to make since the guiding choice has already been made."

Milan spoke quietly, but deeply from the heart: "I want to know more about Eternalism."

"So do I! But what's important now is that we collectively and individually evolve more fully into Attentionists, and get out of the Survivalist hole we're in. One step at a time, Eternalism comes after Attentionism. We need to end the suffering caused by our wrong/right, winner/loser, us/them mentality first.

"Once we do that, we will see, feel, and actualize potentiality that is beyond our current Survivalist imagination. We'll remember we are all aspects of the Source, and our potential to imagine and create will truly and always be infinite. Then life on Earth, or any other planet for that matter, will be very different than what it is now.

"Creating joyfully, sharing playfully, and growing collectively with no fear of lack will take the place of copying and protecting ourselves with fear while suffering."

"What a promising picture Devota. Do you really believe it can come true?"

"Dear Milan, This is not a mere promise or a picture, this is a responsibility that we all have to make real. A responsibility that we have left to institutions and leaders of those institutions. We want the end result, and now as individuals we have to do what it takes to create it for ourselves and others. This is how we arrive at 100% service to self and 100% service to all."

"*100% service to self and 100% service to all,*" Milan repeated. "What a great way of putting it. We usually think of service and self as somehow in conflict with each other. But you have made them one."

common-unity!

Milan leaned back and looked at the greeneries through Devota's spotless glass walls and doors. He imagined the world they described; creating joyfully, sharing playfully, and growing collectively. He felt like a kid exploring an expansive new park. The vistas excited him. With a smile, he turned to his host.

"Back to your story, Devota. It sounds like you lost your community, volunteer work, and previously established relationship with the Source, as you called it. How did you replace them?"

"I did not lose any of them, I upgraded them. Think about the word 'community,' *common-unity*. Once I realized our common unity, interconnectedness, and true story, my community instantly became infinite. All beings are part of my common-unity—some may know it, and some may not know it yet, but they're all part of it. So I did not lose a community, I gained an unlimited community which allows me to connect with anyone from anywhere without a label, pressure, or restriction.

"As for my volunteer work, as a spiritual Attentionist I gained an 'in service' mentality. Which means I work, be it paid or unpaid, with the intention of service. And my relationship with the Source is now more based on love and unity than fear and punishment. In short, community upgraded to common-unity, volunteerism in one institution upgraded to being in service as a way of life, and fear and punishment upgraded to love and oneness. It was worth the struggle, wouldn't you say?"

"*Common-unity*. You Attentionists have a way with words. How would you apply this common-unity if one of your old congregation members showed up in your life again?" Milan asked.

"Well, I would accept them also as part of my common-unity.

However, acceptance is not the same as agreement. I still won't agree with them, assuming their views are the same as before. And I would call them out if I thought they were harming anyone. However, I accept them as they are. Acceptance merely means I see who they are, and respect them by not wanting to override their free will and choice of faith. And I respect myself by continuing my own journey of truth-seeking regardless of their views.

"Which is very different from how they treated me after my departure. I heard a lot of negativity and misinformation about myself, which is expected from any fear-based community. Some members even went out of their way to make life difficult for me, personally and professionally. You see, Survivalists believe if you leave them, you must be bad or wrong, otherwise they are bad or wrong. Same old right/wrong and win/lose situation. Since they don't want to be known as bad or wrong, then you must be the one who takes the blame."

Milan took a moment to let Devota's words settle in. His mind was beginning to feel like a bubbling stew full of unfamiliar and savory ingredients. He smiled at the image, an unusual one for him.

"Respecting their free will and choice even if you don't agree with them. This is yet another new and challenging concept for me, as I'm sure it will be for many others. Boy oh boy if they went after you, that sure sounds like a cult to me."

Devota nodded gently, vestiges of pain evident in their face and words: "Many faith and even so-called spiritual communities think, feel, and act like cults, but those in them see it as unity, not knowing a true union always has room for questioning, exploring, and newness. When we find some subjects/people are not touchable or discussable in our community, then we know we are in a cult, no matter what the group is named or how it has packaged itself."

"To be frank that's why I've never been attracted to such groups," Milan agreed. "They take away your sense of autonomy and curiosity."

"The death of choice, the end of expansion, and limited sharing—three fundamental aspects of our Little-Everything-ness compromised at one go," Devota summarized. "If this is not being a Something, I don't know what is!"

"Amen to that. Now that we share some common views, would you share with me your views on Project Ours?"

Devota took some time before answering. "I understand and respect your innovative idea of moving to a new planet and starting fresh. Of course, a new surrounding, especially a really new surrounding like planet Ours, would be conducive to initial progress. But individual and institutionalized Survivalism are so deeply ingrained in our lives that we don't even see it as a problem, we consider it normal. Over time, old patterns are likely to return and we'll want to escape from planet Ours to planet *Theirs*!

"Attentionism, not for the few but the many, would prevent that. As Attentionists, we can choose unity over separation. We can reconnect with Spirit and soul. And we can put our innovative genius to work on behalf of life and the good of the whole. Innovation without a soul/Spirit connection is a very dangerous gift indeed. We've seen that again and again with everything from gun-powder to the atomic bomb to some of the terrifying aspects of AI. Now you are blazing a trail across the cosmos. But it's not merely a new place that will end our suffering and give us a new chance and superior life. It's a new consciousness and frequency, one that allows us to enjoy a new world, and whatever marvels our wizardly minds come up with, at a higher level. We need to elevate within as we innovate without. Otherwise, new worlds and new technologies will come to naught."

Milan sat pensively with Devota's words and thoughts. A new-found sense of gravity welled up in him. He sat like this for a long minute, until the sound of laughter drifted in from the street. Milan and Devota looked at each other and waited. It was a familiar intrusion. An epidemic of strange laughter had spread like a pandemic throughout the world. It sounded like deep hilarity, but there was an edge of madness in it, the laughter that a crazy person might produce as a last line of defense. Pundits and poets worried about this more than challenging temperatures, vanishing water, and toxic food. It was a frightening breakdown of something deep in the human fabric—the essential lightness of humor hijacked into a voice of insanity, the fearful human pursuit of happiness gone alarmingly awry.

"Of all the things that are happening on the planet, I find this the most disturbing," Milan shared.

"Yes, I am afraid there is an ghastly reality in this unhealthy laughter. But I also know that a bigger truth will ultimately prevail."

"May it be so. You've given me so much to think about, Devota. Deepest thanks. Is there anything else you think I should know before I go?"

"No, I believe I have said enough, and I need to be on my way. I teach a weekly virtual class called *The Art of Dying & Ending* to interested global community members as part of my service. It is a free class and thousands of people from around the globe participate every week."

"*The Art of Dying and Ending*? Oh, so you still are helping people to die?"

"No, I do the opposite, I used to help people die well, and now I help people live well, by showing them death in its true light. You know death is the most feared and least understood experience.

It is a truth that we dread and deny. We think the opposite of death is life, whereas the opposite of death is birth. And life has no opposites, it has been, it is, and it always will be, just as we will always be part of Big-Everything.

"Once we see death from the soul/Spirit perspective, it fundamentally changes the way we lead our lives. Interestingly, this new way of seeing death affects how we see other smaller endings and changes in our life; changing a job, ending a relationship, letting go of experiences that no longer serve us. Endings petrify us as they probably remind us of death, our death."

Milan couldn't help himself: "Tell me more about seeing death from the non-soul/Spirit and the soul/Spirit perspectives."

Devota smiled: "Milan, you are voracious! The former is looking at death from our limited state of physicality, as a true end of what we believe we are—a mere physical being. The small i, as a physical, separated, limited entity, dies and ends. That is a petrifying experience and thought, as it has no memory of dying and coming to life again.

"On the other hand, looking at death from a vaster state of consciousness and energy, it becomes an end of one journey and the beginning of another. Our connection to the Source never ends, and through that we carry the memory of many experiences of death and birth, and hence no fear of ending our current physical experience. Experiences come to an end, but, as a spark of divine energy, we do not. If you ask your expert scientists they'll tell you that energy never dies, it only changes form."

"So your class should be called *The Art of Living*," Milan proposed, a joyful light in his eyes.

"The art of dying, the art of living, two sides of the same coin, one cannot be without the other."

And with that, Devota gracefully got up with a smile and left the room. Milan sat in an unfamiliar silence. The room felt spacious, strongly and strangely so. He practiced what he had learned from his Attentionist friends. He imagined abundance, letting go of focusing on what he had accumulated for Project Ours. He stood at the Observation-Deck and examined his options in that moment. He moved with curiosity to the Neutral-Room to explore his feelings about death informationally, not emotionally. But what still puzzled him was the electricity that kept running through his body in such a strangely unfamiliar and exciting way.

He wondered about living as an Attentionist at all levels and in all the ways he had learned about and discussed. How would people change if they realized the value of their attention, the power of their choice, and could navigate them both intentionally? How would they live differently if they learned what he had learned since meeting Matria and her students? What would the world be like if people shifted from Somethings to Little-Everythings? Milan felt a surge of respect for Devota, who had such a thirst for the truth and paid a high price to explore it. He found himself also pondering and wondering about the truth. It amazed him that he was paying *his* attention to things he had never been conscious of before, and he realized in that moment that somehow, Project Ours did not stand on the top of his list anymore.

… As Milan got up and left Devota's home, he asked himself out-loud: *What's happening inside of me? What is this energy that makes me want to cry, and dance?*

re-

union

9

For Milan, meeting Devota was peculiar and outside his realm. Nevertheless, he was deeply interested in the subjects they spoke about: Spirit vs. soul, spirituality vs. religiosity, a relational vs. transactional connection to the Source, and most importantly, truth vs. reality.

The electricity Milan felt at the end of his meeting with Devota came back each day after he returned home. It was a strange, exciting feeling, as if energy that had been locked up for a long time had been released. This energy, coupled with Devota's words and an unfamiliar yearning, made Milan curious about his own spirituality. He wondered why his family had been uninterested in the subject. His parents and relatives discussed political, artistic, and traditional aspects of their religious background, but nothing more. With one exception. He dimly remembered his grandmother, with whom he was close, praying and speaking about her deep relationship with God.

Milan allowed the subject to stay alive for him and revisited it whenever he found time alone. He felt like something new in him was being born, and he attended to it like a secret love, this newfound sense of spirituality, and the tingling inside.

He decided to ask his family about his grandmother. He wondered why he remembered events before and after her death but not much about the death itself. His mother helped him understand: "After grandma passed away, you stopped talking about her altogether," she told him. "It seemed like her death was too much for you at such a young age, so we went along with it and never talked about her in front of you again." Milan teared up as he left the conversation with his mother—an unfamiliar experience for him, but one that had happened a few times since his meetings with Matria and her friends.

I remember grandma, I remember her love for me, and I remember her love for God, he thought. *The last time I remember being with her was when I was going through a painful experience as a child—my best friend was seriously ill—and she put me on her lap and told me to pray and let God resolve it for me. But not long after, grandma died, and my problem wasn't resolved; in fact, not long after that, my friend was also gone.*

Milan suddenly went still. *That's when… when my sulking relationship with God began! Oh my God, I remember vividly now. I cut ties with God and my memories of grandma, who was the only person who spoke about God, and the only close loved one, beside my friend, who died when I was young.* Milan was sobbing as these memories surged back.

He stayed in his room for days. He cried, he laughed, he felt sadness, relief, wonder, confusion, joy. *How could I have filed away all these memories as a kid?* he asked himself, amazed. When Milan finally came out of his room and returned to everyday life, he experienced himself quite differently. He felt liberated somehow, lighter, freer, more able to explore his relationship with the invisible world of energy, and the Big-Everything, as Matria called it.

Milan's expertise was in expanding and pushing the boundaries of the *yeki-bood*, the visible realm of life, and now he had developed a deep fascination for the *yeki-nabood*, the invisible realm. He noticed that he felt electricity every time he paid attention to the *yeki-nabood*. This current of energy intimated the existence of Big-Everything in his mind.

Will my newfound relationship with the invisible realm help heal my troubled relationships in the visible one? Milan wondered.

kuriozi wants to know

After a few days, Milan decided to see Matria again and somehow make sense of the puzzling, unfamiliar road he was on. He felt like he wanted to take Kuriozi with him, so he asked if she was interested. Kuriozi lit up at the question, but she had a couple of her own.

"I'm so excited to go with you and see Matria again, but I want to know why we're going back to see her. Did you meet with the people she recommended?"

"Yes, I did."

"And?"

"What do you want to know?"

"I want to know what you learned about Attentionism. And by the way, is that why you've been weird lately?"

Milan laughed, enjoying the coded compliment from his daughter: "Weird, what do you mean? I'm just a bit more contemplative these days."

"There, even you using that word is weird. I've never seen you contemplating. You think a lot, but you don't contemplate."

"How do you distinguish between contemplating and thinking?" Milan asked.

Kuriozi answered without missing a beat: "Contemplation is like traveling to discover the globe, and thinking is like traveling to a specific and small place in the world."

Milan shook his head. "It's astonishing how much you know. I'm so impressed by you. Alright, let me share what I learned from the people Matria directed me to meet. Are you ready?"

"I am."

"OK. I met four different Attentionists: Sukseso, a physical Attentionist, Menso, a mental Attentionist, Lamenti, an emotional

Attentionist, and Devota, a spiritual Attentionist. Meeting and speaking with them, I realized I had, *ahem,* overlooked a few key points in my plan to build a more advanced life on planet Ours. And I am, as you know, one of the smartest people on planet Earth!"

"Lol, even though you say so, Dad. Just kidding, I think you're very smart, and now you're becoming wise."

"Actually, I'm realizing how wise *you* are, Kuriozi. How many classes do you have with Matria each week?"

"Just one. But it's not because I see Matria a lot that I learn from her, it's the way she teaches. She tells us stories and makes it fun. We don't feel like we're in a class learning, we think we're in a playground playing with words, colors, shapes, numbers, and stories. Also, she treats us like we're important and we matter. She listens to every word we say and every question we ask. She reminds us constantly how valuable and wise we are. She takes us into nature and invites us to connect with the elementals. When we ask her a question, she asks it back and says we already know the answer. She has taught us to balance the four elements of fire, air, earth and water, by remembering the fifth element—love. She truly sees and treats us as if we're Little-Everythings, like in the story she told us when we first went to her house."

Milan went quiet and identified something new about his interaction with Kuriozi. He was talking to her as if she and what she had to say mattered. It was strange to realize that even though he loved his daughter deeply, he had never really thought what she believed or had to say was worthy of his attention. He always thought of her as just a child, a teenager. But now, seeing her through Attentionist eyes, he found her to be a fascinating, deep, inquisitive human being with interesting views.

Kuriozi sensed her dad's inner shift, and decided to take a chance—a huge one that she'd been holding onto for a long time. "And I truly hope you learn from Matria and treat me the same way. I've felt unseen and unimportant since Mom took her life."

Milan stiffened. "What do you mean took her life? Sky passed away naturally."

"Dad, please stop pretending. *I* know, *you* know, Mother did not die of natural causes; she took her life. Probably because she was unseen and unheard, like I am, only for a much longer time."

Milan was instantly clotted with outrage and shock. He couldn't believe what he had just heard: "Are you saying I killed her by not hearing or seeing her? If that would kill people, most of us wouldn't make it to adulthood."

Milan was so rattled that he did not know what to do or how to proceed with Kuriozi. He thought he was doing better than before, and now this!

The charged energy of the room was heavy and seemingly unresolvable. Until Milan remembered his conversation with Lamenti, and the silences they sometimes shared. He gave himself room to be silent now—he sensed that Kuriozi would be ok with it—and started tuning into his emotions informationally, through the very loud bellhops who were seeking him out. He began to calm down as he got their messages and realized that his desire and intention was for love and connection with Kuriozi… and that he was far from either at the moment.

Lamenti's teaching on energy and matter, which Milan had resisted at the time, suddenly came to mind. *I wonder if I can apply this now?* he asked himself, as Kuriozi waited and watched. *The matter I'm seeking, or was seeking before I was called a murderer, is to share my learnings with Kuriozi. And the energy that will take me there is, I don't know, perhaps, I suppose, service or love or joy of sharing. Let me see, joy… is too far from where I am. Love… of course I love her but I'm not feeling loving right now after the accusation I just heard. But service is accessible to me in this moment. Serving a child, my child, who has lived with a terrifying secret of knowing her mother took her life instead of mothering her… is easy.*

Milan began to un-clench and relax. His rage softened, and he took a few long breaths with the intention of serving and nourishing himself. *What I do not have, I cannot share, so I need to take care of and serve myself first and foremost.*

Milan realized he was in Lamenti's Neutral-Room, processing emotions as information, connecting to his own sense of choice. He floated in this space for a while, trusting the stillness of the moment, until something shifted inside and he felt ready to reconnect with Kuriozi, to share in service in whatever way came up. He felt no discomfort, even though the rough exchanges of a few moments ago were still vivid in his mind. He felt like he was on a higher floor watching himself elevate from Rational-Mind to Whole-Mind. He was confused about how all these experiences were interconnected, but he was also aware that he was experiencing a level beyond his norms of attack and defend.

His heart suddenly opened, and, without thinking, Milan approached Kuriozi, knelt down, and softly asked, "May I hold you?"

Kuriozi, stunned by this unexpected turn, quietly murmured, "Yes, Dad. I've been waiting for you to ask me this for years." Then, tears began to stream down her face. They grew into quiet crying, which swelled into sobbing, then wailing, before subsiding into exhaustion.

Milan held Kuriozi close, saying nothing. He allowed his energy to speak for him—energy that had transformed in silence from anger, to neutrality, to self-care, to service, and finally to love for Kuriozi. It all felt natural.

Kuriozi, drained by the overwhelming release of long-suppressed emotions, remained in her father's arms. Her mind briefly recalled falling asleep in the arms of countless nannies, and, much earlier, in her mother's embrace—but never in Milan's.

Milan and Kuriozi ended their challenging day with a long goodnight hug before retreating to their bedrooms and seeking refuge in the arms of sleep.

As they parted, Milan said, "Tomorrow, I'll share what I've learned with you, my dear Kuriozi. In fact, I'll take the whole day off so we can spend it together—just the two of us."

Kuriozi, still in a state of disbelief, nodded silently. As she opened the door to her room, Milan suddenly turned back, his voice trembling as he said, "I am so deeply sorry for all the pain I've caused you."

For the first time in her life, Kuriozi saw her father cry—truly cry—his tears flowing freely, unrestrained. Overwhelmed, she rushed toward him, wrapping him in her arms to console him. In that moment, their roles seemed to reverse. Kuriozi held Milan with the tenderness and wisdom of a loving parent. To her surprise, she felt no resentment, only compassion. It was as if her purpose had been to teach her father something profound—and she had just fulfilled it.

Kuriozi softly said, "I see that, Dad. Thank you for your tears."

And that was all. No more words were needed. Both of them felt an unspoken shift, a quiet transformation in their bond.

As the night deepened, the darkness seemed to cradle the light of this newfound realization. Their house, for the first time, felt like a home—a space filled with love and the silent promise of a new beginning.

morning

Father and daughter both slept deeply and peacefully that night, waking up refreshed. By some delightful coincidence, they arrived in the kitchen at nearly the same moment, laughing as they caught sight of each other entering from opposite sides.

They decided to make breakfast together—yet another unprecedented event. The morning felt unusually bright, as if the day itself had come to mirror their transformation. They enjoyed an unrushed meal on the terrace, soaking in the sun, and each other's company.

When the time felt right, Milan gently pulled back Kuriozi's chair for her to stand, and hand-in-hand they made their way to the conference room next to the library. Kuriozi skipped lightly, her joy uncontainable, while Milan moved with a calm, steady flow.

Once seated, Milan lovingly began: *"Now,* dear Kuriozi, let me share with you what I've learned from the Attentionists. I first met with Sukseso, the physical Attentionist. They had been through a remarkable journey, and they taught me three major things about this realm:

"Like Matria, they said there are two worlds—the visible and the invisible- but they explained that each world has its own currency. The currency of the visible world is money, and the currency of the invisible world is attention. Attention is more valuable than money because it plays a stronger role in determining how happy and healthy we are in life. What we pay attention to is what we make ours, so we need to pay attention to what we pay attention to!

"Second, they taught me the difference between accumulation and abundance. My daughter, this alone was worth my entire journey. In survival we accumulate and 'produce,' and in choice we feel abundant and 'create.' True abundance comes from intentionality and knowing that we can experience whatever we want—not from merely possessing more.

"Lastly, Sukseso taught me about MMD, or the More & More Disease, which is the widespread, uncontrollable, addictive urge to accumulate. It's a clear sign we are operating in survival mode rather than a place of choice—regardless of how much we own or know.

"I wonder if you can relate to any of this, Kuriozi?" Milan smiled broadly. "Of course you can. Somehow you have known these things all along. Anyway, Sukseso sent me to Menso, the mental Attentionist, another extraordinary person, who taught me the following about the mind:

"First, Menso explained that the mind has many moving parts, but broadly speaking, three aspects stand out: the Rational-Mind, the Whole-Mind, and a bridge between the two called the Observation-Deck.

"Second, each part of the mind has a job. The job of the Rational-Mind, especially in the survivalist state, is to separate and protect us in the physical world. The job of the Whole-Mind, which includes rationality but goes far beyond it, is to give us larger access to the wider world and help us create, like when we were Little-Everythings. And the Observation-Deck helps us see and remember we have a choice beyond old conditioning and survival.

"Last, Menso shared the startling insight that imagination and worry are closely related. Imagination is thinking gone lovingly infinite, while worry is imagination gone negative and dark. In survival mode, we worry excessively about painful past experiences, or imagined future ones. In a state of choice, we use imagination to dream of new and helpful possibilities."

Milan paused to see how his audience was holding up. Not to

worry. Kuriozi was hanging on every word, as if Milan was sharing tales from *The Arabian Nights*. He continued:

"Menso then sent me to Lamenti, the emotional Attentionist. They too had an incredible journey and taught me things I especially needed to learn about our emotions and energetic life:

"Number one, there is a basic structure in life called the Triangle-of-Self: who and how we are and feel is shaped by a triad of genes, history, and choice. Most of us remain victims of our genes and history, rarely activating our true power of choice—except within the narrow confines of survival.

"Second, e-motions, as the word indicates, are Energy in Motion: When emotions arise shaking their bell like bellhops, we need to create a pause and invite them into the Neutral-Room. There we meet them and use their message as a barometer to measure how close or far we are from what we'd like to feel. Emotions become informational tools for self-awareness, well-being, and choice, enabling us to become emotionally independent rather than emotional beggars.

"Third, balancing energy is the secret to a healthy emotional life. Each of us contain both feminine and masculine energies regardless of biology or gender identity. As emotional Attentionists, we use these energies in a balanced way, depending on what is needed. In this harmonious state, our heart creates and our mind implements. Together, they give birth to experiences that allow us to live happily as Little-Everythings in the Somethings' world.

"Kuriozi, after meeting with Sukseso, Menso and Lamenti, I was flying high, and eager to meet Devota, the spiritual Attentionist. I doubt that I would have agreed to visit Devota at the beginning of my journey. But it turned out to be a real highlight. They taught me the following about the spiritual realm:

"First, truth and reality are not necessarily the same. Truth is one, but reality is our version of the truth, which may or may not be the truth or the whole truth. When our reality is far from the truth, our relationship with the Divine becomes transactional instead of connectional. When true connection is made, the pure pleasure of becoming one and aligned with the Divine becomes a pleasure in itself, and free from any qualifications or conditions.

"Second, what Devota called Survivalist spirituality is often behind the troubling aspects of institutional religion. When soul enters the realms of fear and Survivalism, it can become dense, defensive, or even adversarial, attacking other forms of spirituality or contradicting its own essence. At times, it may morph into an institution that prioritizes its own survival over the very truth it was founded to uphold, obscuring the light it was meant to share.

"Last but not least, Kuriozi, consciousness is the key. The true change I'm looking to take to planet *Ours* is not about innovations, inventions, and technologies that can either improve or degrade the quality of life. And it's not just about better ways to manage our bodies, hearts, and minds. It's about the elevation of consciousness, the connection to Spirit and soul, which opens the door more widely and allows innovation to turn into creation, and serve life."

Milan finished, exhausted and elated by all he had unpacked. Kuriozi felt intensely proud to be part of her dad's journey. "Wow," she said, shaking her head. "You've learned so much just by meeting four people. And boy, did you have a lot to learn!"

Milan nodded, smiling deeply. "I know, it's amazing what you can learn from others in such a short time, when they..."

"When they what?" Kuriozi prompted, leaning in.

Milan's smile stretched even further. "When they have high AQ."

Kuriozi burst out laughing. "Dad, you're sounding more and

more like Matria. Are you okay with that?"

"I guess I'm going to have to be," Milan replied, looking anything but unhappy. "But I have to go now and be in silence in order to connect with myself. Be ready by 3:00 p.m. tomorrow, kiddo. We're going to see Matria again. This time, I'll have a better idea of what to expect… *I think*."

Kuriozi tilted her head. "What about my other question? Why are you going back to see Matria?"

Milan shrugged, with the pleasure of not knowing. "Honestly, I'm not exactly sure. But I'm excited anyway. It's a new feeling for me—being happy about something without knowing why."

"Oh, I know that feeling well," Kuriozi said, her eyes sparkling. "And I love it. It's like being part of life *and* excited about life at the same time. Just life. I can't wait to see the new you in the company of Matria."

re-union

Driving to Matria with Kuriozi felt different this time around. A quiet connection filled the space between them—a bond, a depth, and an ease that hadn't been there during their earlier trip. Milan took pauses and felt comfortable with silence. There was no loud music in the way. He paid attention to greeneries, people on the road, and more importantly to what was going on inside of him. He was also more present and curious about Kuriozi. He drove with pleasure and a gentle smile on his face.

They arrived on time, and Matria opened the door with a big smile. She hugged Kuriozi first and then she waited to see if Milan was ready for the same. Milan was not a hugger, but he went for Matria's open arms and they shared a surprisingly long embrace, so long that Kuriozi began to wonder if she had to step in and separate the two manually. They sat around the table that Matria had set with fruits and herbal teas, and enjoyed being together without saying a word. Finally, Matria turned to Milan with a mischievous look, and asked about his encounters with her Attentionist friends.

"So, how did your meetings go?"

"As if you don't know," Milan replied with a laugh. "Haven't your pals told you all about it."

Matria chuckled. "I have spoken with them, but dear Milan, surely you've noticed that people rarely describe the same event the same way. We each have our own focus, our own intentions. I'm more interested in what you have to say."

"Ah yes, it's like the story of the elephant that Devota told me about. The meetings were amazing, Matria. They changed me, so much so that I now feel like I need to unfold something more before I can go further in my project. But I don't know what exactly it is. I'm hoping you can help me figure it out?"

Matria looked at Milan thoughtfully: "Unfolding is a tremendous journey for any being. Remember that our whole story started by Big-Everything unfolding Itself. However, I invite you to clarify your question so that I can answer it more helpfully."

"OK, how about this. I'm not sure it's the best question, but it's clear and direct: What are your views about my project of wanting to create another home for humanity on planet Ours?"

"I like your word *create*," Matria replied. "Hold on to it for now. But let me answer your question with a question—*why* do you want to create life for Earthlings on planet Ours? I mean truly why? I'm not looking for the answers you may give to the media, but the one that you know comes from inside of you, your true intention."

Milan hesitated: "I want to colonize planet Ours and make it habitable for our people. Funny, I'm feeling uncomfortable as I say 'colonize,' but have no idea why. I've been using this word since I started thinking and talking about Ours, but it no longer feels right."

Matria gazed at Milan warmly: "You have changed, Milan. And as our consciousness changes, so does our vocabulary. Survivalist words like colonization don't fit our Attentionist heart/mind anymore. But back to my question—Why do you want to go to planet Ours? Your answer was about *what* you want to do, I asked you *why* do you want to do it?"

"Because..." Milan quickly began, then caught himself, closed his eyes, and took a few breaths. "...Because I believe we have messed up this planet so badly that we need to become multi-planetary with a choice about where we want to live."

"Oh, choice, I agree with that," Matria said. "Now let's unfold it a bit. Don't you think the choice of where to live is really about being happier and having more meaning?"

"Please elaborate, Matria."

Kuriozi jumped in without any invitation and offered her services: "Matria, I understand, can I explain it please?"

"Go right ahead, dear."

Kuriozi beamed: "We want to have a choice of where to live, because having a choice makes us happier and freer and we like that. So asking which planet do I want to live on is not so much about a location as about how we want to be. I mean, it's more about being than doing, right, Matria?"

"Absolutely, Kuriozi. Well put."

"Thank you, Kuriozi," Milan said, taking in his daughter with pride. "Okay, let's say the choice is about how to be happier, which includes but is not limited to the question of where in the cosmos we want to live. How does that affect and change my project?"

"Let's change your question even further and see what happens," Matria pressed, "because when we change our question we change our journey, and a larger piece of the truth may become available. So if your question becomes "What can I create to help people of Earth be happier…?"

Milan interrupted: "But don't I first need to identify why people aren't happy?"

"Yes, good, let's go there. Why do you think at a deeper and more fundamental level people are suffering?"

Again, Kuriozi jumped in: "I know why, because they are separated from each other and they have forgotten they're made out of love, not fear."

"And because they are really Little-Everythings, living as if they're Somethings!" Milan completed, the words escaping as if of their own accord.

He clapped a hand over his mouth, startled by the simplicity his realization, and the language that he used. A creamy silence enveloped the room. Each person sat quietly, savoring the connection they had cultivated and now shared. Kuriozi bit into an apple, Matria closed her eyes and sipped her herbal tea, and Milan, with deliberate care, began peeling an orange, embodying the mindful presence they all embraced.

multi-dimensional or multi-planetary

After a few minutes, Milan broke the silence with another realization.

"Basically, adult Earthlings need to be un-taught Survivalism and taught Attentionism, and youngsters need to not be taught Survivalist programming but encouraged to stay curious and connected to the Source; that way all of us can gradually remember the unlimited and united beings that we once were."

Kuriozi and Matria smiled. Milan thought to himself: *Was it really just a few short weeks since I flinched with impatience as Matria unfolded her* Story *and ideas?*

Then, turning to Matria, he continued: "But back to my questions—what about multi-planetary choices? Where does that fit in?"

"Once we realize our multi-dimensional choices, multi-planetary choices will also be satisfied," she replied. "You see, one hundred includes ninety, but ninety does not include one hundred. Do you understand what I mean?"

"I do, Matria, I do. But how do we access our multi-dimensionality?"

"Person-by-person, step-by-step. We were designed and created based on an original blueprint. When our consciousness fell—when separation, fear, and polarity became our reality—many functions of our bodies, minds, and hearts stopped working or began to malfunction. Our lesser consciousness had no use for them. As one of us remembers and reactivates, we make it easier for others to do the same. We just need to focus on discovering our multi-dimensionality. As we do, the next step will reveal itself naturally."

Milan leaned back, considering her words. "So, in other words, if we choose to pay attention—intentionally—appropriate actions will follow?"

"Yes. But remember, paying attention is also an act, an act of being as well as doing. Energy as well as matter, as I'm sure you've heard."

Milan sighed, a mixture of clarity and hesitation in his face. "I have not forgotten. But I still have major questions before I can decide how—or even if—I want to move ahead with my project."

Matria looked at Milan gently: "Are you making up your mind, Milan, or connecting your mind to your heart?"

"Oh, Matria, I've never been as connected to my heart as I am now. I decide with my heart and implement with my mind." Then, turning to Kuriozi: "When I look at you, Kuriozi, my heart and mind connect instantly. My love for you is now my guide."

Kuriozi's eyes filled. Matria too was moved. The seeds of a profound journey were taking root.

attentionism or eternalism?

"Please continue, Milan," Matria prodded. "I love the path you're taking with this."

"With pleasure, Matria. But I have another question that's been bugging me for some time. If you love this path, then why don't we take it all the way to Eternalism instead of Attentionism? Isn't that a higher state?"

"Dear Milan, even in the invisible realm, your ambition shines through. The distance between Survivalism and Eternalism is vast. If we try to bridge it too quickly, we risk backtracking or delaying the process. Think of it this way: we need to learn the alphabet of Attentionism and choice-making before we can write the book of Eternalism."

Milan sighed with mock frustration: "Are you saying Attentionism is a necessary state between Survivalism and Eternalism?"

"Yes. There are some exceptions both historically and presently, and they can become the norm once we collectively practice choice. We're getting closer. The wisdom that was available to a few in the past is now available to all. That's because many desired, practiced, and created what we're looking for. They paved the way for us. Just like when an athlete breaks a record and that then becomes the norm for the rest. Awaking from the sleep, or, more accurately, the nightmare of Survivalism, has started and there's a lot of help for those who choose to wake up."

Milan listened with a curious expression on his face. There was something else he wanted to ask, but he wasn't sure how.

"Matria, may I pose a personal question? Did you come to this world as the Eternalist I see before me now?"

Matria smiled, a flicker of nostalgia and pain in her gaze. She took her time before answering. "No, not by a long shot. I was born in a troubled and unwelcoming environment. I learned early in life that I had to take care of myself. I reached out to my imagination, which was vivid, for help and comfort. It gifted me with an uncanny relationship with the invisible world.

"I talked to God as if they were a person. I had no training or idea who God was, and I still don't, but I was hungry for a connection to the beyond, because what was before me was deeply dissatisfying.

"I have lived many lives in this one physical life. I lost people and things as I moved around the globe and started over again and again. I felt homeless, yet at home wherever I lived. Like most people, I suffered and caused suffering, until it hurt so much that I realized I had to find a different way of leading my life.

"And then I remembered I was happiest when I was a child. Not because I had a happy childhood or a healthy environment, but because I was connected and closer to the Source, in charge of my attention, and intentional in my imagination, and hence my actions.

"I remembered making time as a child for connection to what I had left behind to arrive here, going on the roof at night, gazing at the stars and reaching out to a consciousness beyond mine.

"I realized my solace was in remembering, imagining, and desiring to be *here* but feel like I felt *there*, in the Land-of-Unity. We spoke before about how we arrive in this physical life connected naturally as Little-Everythings. We then get trained and conditioned into denseness and Something-*ness* and become deeply attached to physicality. However, if we so choose, we can bring this cycle to an end at exactly the same place we started, as connected Little-Everythings, by choice this time, not nature.

"Eventually, I made it my intention to do just that and share what I know with those who decide to stop their suffering. I have had many students but not all of them took the teachings into their life. They loved the words and forgot the living."

Matria finished as she began, with a smile, and a hint of shadow that could still be detected on her normally light-filled face.

Milan was riveted. But after a moment he pressed: "So is there such a thing as a chosen Eternalist?"

"We are all chosen Eternalists, my dear, but some assembly is required on our part, and we need to choose to activate our chosen-ness. Do you see that choice and free will are the key to all of this?"

choice and free will

"Yes, I do," Milan affirmed with an ease that surprised him. He would not have known how to answer before Kuriozi hooked him up with her teacher and changed his life. "My choice, and everyone else's. But Matria, you told me the story of initial creation and how things began. Can you now tell me the story of choice and how things will end? The final story?"

"*The Story* will never end, Milan. We will continue using our free will for the purpose of expanding, exploring and experiencing as the creative beings that we are. Eventually, every single Something will return to being a Little-Everything.

"Every single Something?"

"Yes, every Something, even those who seem far from that now. The question is will it be sooner or later, and how much suffering is enough before we choose liberation."

"Just like that, open the door? Can we really? Is it that simple?"

"The question is *will,* not can. Will comes before can, intention before action. When we will, we can!"

Milan considered: "So that's all we need, intention and action?"

"Attention, intention and action," Matria clarified. "We need to pay attention to our intention and act accordingly. Attention is the link, the mediator, the determining factor. For instance, the difference between you and those in your world—your classmates, neighbors, siblings—is what you mainly pay attention to; one may pay more attention to form and fashion, or to copying others, or to accumulating wealth. But you, you want to create a new world."

"I do, and the question is am I doing it right?"

am i doing it right?

Matria clapped her hands and bowed her head lightly. "*Thank you.* Now you're asking the right question. Your intention is to create a new and better world. Your action, however, is to take over planet Ours. Let's bring our attention to the words 'creation' and 'conquest.' Do they speak to each other? Are they from the same family, energy, consciousness?"

Milan thought for a moment: "Are you saying intention and action need to be made of the same material, so to speak?"

"Exactly. Attention, intention and action all need to be made of the same vibration, or material as you put it. If I want love, and my attention is on control, and my action is harsh, do you think I'll be loving or loved? Often when things don't go the way we want, it's because our intention, attention, and action, or any combination of these three, are not cohesive. You want the members of this triangle to cooperate, not compete."

Milan smiled as if from an internal *aha*. "In that case, the answer is *no*. Creation is from the Eternalist world and conquest from the Survivalist one. Especially if it involves subjugating beings who may already live on a planet they call home." Milan smiled, and glanced at Kuriozi. "It's amazing how things clear up when you ask the right question. But Matria, back to square one, how then do I create a better new world?"

Matria laughed as if it wasn't really all that hard: "Remember our Creation Story? The Little-Everythings created universes, multiverses, megaverses. We are creator beings who have forgotten our creative abilities, so at best we take over already existing things and make them ours—no pun intended—instead of creating new things that can be uniquely and joyfully ours!"

Milan's head fell to his chest, but he was smiling: "Are you suggesting I create a new world here instead of migrating to planet Ours? That seems much harder!"

"I'm saying you need to decide which action is closest to your intention," Matria replied. "This is your decision, not mine. And you need to align your triangle or you will not feel satisfied no matter which planet you live on."

final question

Milan sipped his tea thoughtfully. There was no hurry in the room. Silence continued to play an important role in the conversation. Finally, he picked up the thread.

"Matria, I have one more question to help me decide whether I want to help humanity become multi-planetary or multi-dimensionary."

Kuriozi did a double take: "Multi-dimensionary. Dad, are you making up words now too?"

All three laughed.

"It's contagious," Milan said, with a helpless and happy shrug. "But seriously, if I decide to do the latter, I'll need the guidance and leadership of an Attentionist who has gone through this transformation, understands the suffering of Survivalists, the freedom of Attentionists, and the potential joy of the Eternalist state. Someone who has learned Attentionism at many levels—physical, mental, emotional, and spiritual. Someone who has the passion and drive to help humanity experience, express, and expand itself. Someone who wants to grow and be of service to others so that they can do the same. An extraordinary person who does not want to settle for ordinary and can help make extra-ordinary ordinary. I know this is a tall order, but do you know anyone with these qualifications or close to them who can help me in Project Ours?"

Matria went quiet as if going through her invisible list to find that person, then she gently turned toward Kuriozi and asked: "Kuriozi, since you've already played a marvelous role as connector and match-maker in your dad's project, can you think of anyone?"

Kuriozi's playful face and wide smile came before her words: "You mean beside my dad himself?"

Milan laughed: "…Very funny, *ha ha ha*…."

A teasing silence filled the room.

"You're kidding, right?" Milan reddened, then straightened up. "Matria, do you really think I qualify for all that I just described?"

Matria looked at Milan with serious regard: "I do. Your aim, now that it has changed from survival and take-over to creation and expansion in service to Earth and beyond, qualifies you. And you'll have the support of all kinds of Attentionists and Eternalists around, above, and throughout the globe once you initiate your creation. Who knows, you may even get help from some Darlings!

"There are so many extraordinary beings living ordinary lives among us. All you need is to want to meet them, and there they will be. The researcher you needed to help you find a teacher was living in your own home—Kuriozi—and she was a heart-connector, not a head-hunter. And the person you were seeking to elevate your project? He was within you all along. When you were ready, he showed up, didn't he?"

Milan hesitated, then smiled: "Looks like he did, at least more than I imagined."

Matria continued: "As Rumi, an Eternalist who once lived on Earth, says, '*the Sorahi, the jug of water, is sitting in my home, and here I am wandering around the globe in thirst and in search of water!*' Go and drink from the waters within, as your miraculous self contains the fountain of all you're searching for. And as you become more of a Little-Everything and less of a Something, you'll be amazed at the miracles that move around and through you."

Milan exhaled deeply. "I appreciate your encouragement,

Matria, and I think I know what *you* believe I should do. But this project has been my passion for so long—I need to consider all options. Here's another question: Let's say I go to Ours with a healthy intention. How can I know the Ourians will be willing to connect, collaborate, and cooperate? What if they share the same colonizing ambitions I had before, and they too are living in survival mode?"

"I can assure you they're looking for connection and want to help Earthlings elevate."

"How can you be sure?"

"I can be sure because I know Ourians have already shared what they know with those Earthlings who want to know."

Milan and Kuriozi exchanged looks, as if to say, *"Did she just say what I think she said?"* Then Milan looked at Matria.

"How do you know this, Matria? And is it knowledge or knowing?"

"Both."

Milan leaned forward and locked eyes with Matria: "Please elaborate."

Matria took a deep breath, and smiled: "I had a knowing when I lived as an *Ourian*, and wanted to connect and share with Earthlings. I trusted that deep knowing. And now that I'm here living on Earth, I have knowledge and experience of it first-hand."

Slowly, carefully, Milan put down his cup of tea. Kuriozi looked at her dad and put her hand on her mouth. They both stopped breathing for a few seconds.

"Matria… am I hearing this right, are you saying that you are an *Ourian* living on Earth?" Milan asked.

"That is what I am saying, dear ones. I know it is a shock, but a necessary one to help you decide how to proceed."

Again, silence took over the room, this time like a strangely glowing mist. Milan went into a daze. Kuriozi's eyes and smile widened as much as humanly possible. And Matria held the space with an other-worldly energy of love.

"Matria, my head is bursting with questions..."

"...and I can't believe my teacher, Matria, is from another planet!"

"There is much to feel and explore here, let's be gentle," Matria counseled.

Milan put his hands on his temples, and, remembering Lamenti, started humming to take himself out of fear. He then chose excitement as his primary feeling. Kuriozi, filled with curiosity, stared at Matria with an intensity that far surpassed her years. Matria placed her hand over her heart, grounding herself, and the room. "Matria is an *Ourian,* the very planet I wanted to colonize," Milan mumbled, to no one in particular. Kuriozi and Matria held the complexity of the moment in silence. The room felt unfamiliar, yet eerily intimate.

Finally, Milan eased out of his state of shock. "You told me all about your Earth experience Matria, how did that happen then?" he asked. "I can't fathom your story now."

"The mind can't fathom what it has not yet experienced," she replied. "Go to your heart and allow my words to settle there. To answer your question, I volunteered to come to Earth and go through the pains of birth and life of an Earthling, with the intention of aiding those who choose to remember who they are and where they have come from beyond their limited Earth experiences. I knew I could not initiate your journeys, but I could assist them."

"Did you know all along that you were an *Ourian* living on Earth?"

"I had a feeling that I was different and gradually I remembered more and more. My hint was being different. I know being different may be considered a disadvantage here, but for me it was an indication of uniqueness and authenticity. I imagined a lot, I saw and understood things in a different way, I was not interested in following others or being the same as them. I celebrated my so called odd-ness without making it obvious to others. All this helped me remember the why of my journey here faster."

"So you lived here as if you are from here?" Milan asked. "When in Rome do as the Romans do?"

"When in Rome do as the *elevated* Romans do," Matria corrected with a smile.

"And if you can't find an elevated one?"

"Become one!"

"But why? Why go through all that pain?"

"Why do you want to help others on Earth and save them from destruction, Milan? Why don't you just save yourself? Because once you know we all come from the same Source, you realize 'Me' is just 'We', upside down. As the great poet Saadi, another Eternalist who lived on Earth, wrote: *If a body part is afflicted with pain, other body parts uneasy will remain*! Many beings want to help Earth because the Fall-of-Consciousness and rise of destruction on Earth has affected all of existence."

"All of existence?"

"Yes…"

Milan and Kuriozi silently digested this startling new disclosure. Milan never imagined that Earth mattered to the universe. If true, then the cosmos, including the blue marble we call home, is wired beyond Survivalism, and towards interdependence. It's not every planet for itself, he realized, just like it can't be every man for himself.

Kuriozi broke the ruminating lull: "I knew Matria was from somewhere else, I knew it right from the beginning, but I didn't dare to say it because no one would have believed me, or if they did, they might have harmed Matria."

Matria looked lovingly at Kuriozi. She hesitated, not quite sure whether to speak. Then:

"That's true, dear Kuriozi…. You knew because you lack the heaviness of judgment and doubt that clouds so many. And also… because… you, too, once lived on Ours."

Milan and Kurioza froze. Milan with a hint of fear. Kuriozi with unadulterated amazement and joy.

"Oh my God, please stop, Matria. This is too much. My little girl… Kuriozi… is also an *Ourian*?!"

Matria flushed with the new wave of overwhelm she had just sparked: "Yes. She was, and now she is an Earthling—you can be both. And there are many other young ones among you who carry a knowing far beyond the common Earth understanding. They, too, have come to help raise the collective consciousness."

Milan balked: "As captivating as what you just said sounds, right now I am only thinking about my kid. I am floored, thrilled, amused, and also concerned. So the two of you Ourians decided to come and be part of my life, just like that?"

"It is never just like that," Matria replied, as soothingly as possible. "The universe is a match-maker, the best match-maker ever. You decide what you want to experience by paying attention to it, and the universe finds the right people for you to make it happen. Kuriozi must have wanted to be born to an unusual and fascinating father, and you must have wanted to have an unusual daughter and the experiences that come with her. And voila—here you are going through them together."

"But Matria, if I can't remember choosing this, even though I appreciate it now, Who is this *'I'* you speak of?"

"There are many I's in every person. The I who only knows and focuses on the life at hand, the higher I who seeks what's needed for elevation, the collective I who sees all journeys of self and others and knows a much bigger picture of life… and finally the I who arrives at One. So one of your I's beside the obvious must have chosen to have Kuriozi as your daughter and me as your support."

Milan had many feelings and emotions that went beyond words. For the second time in twenty-four hours, he went toward Kuriozi and held her tight. Kuriozi started to cry with joy. She was overtaken by confusing feelings. She asked Matria to join them, and their collective hug formed a triangle.

Milan was shivering as they held each other, but could not stop asking questions. "Do *Ourians* have the same level of Survivalism and suffering as we do on Earth?"

"Yes and no," Matria replied. "Each planet exists at a certain level of consciousness, with individuals who may rise above or fall below the average. There are twelve levels of consciousness as far as I know. Ours collectively operates at a higher level than Earth. There's still plenty of suffering, but not like here. And not as dangerous."

"Out of twelve, where does Earth stand?"

"Earth is at level three but aspires and is able to reach five and beyond."

"Boy oh boy do we have a long way to go!"

"The third dimension is dense, heavy, and addictive," Matria concurred. "It clings to you, making it difficult to move on. But once you begin the journey upward, progress accelerates. Reaching the fifth level from three is far more challenging than going from the fifth to the seventh. The lighter you become, the easier it gets."

"Do I have to do anything differently now that I know I too am an *Ourian*?" Kuriozi asked, her eyes luminous as moons?

"You don't need to change anything, dear one. Simply remember why you're here. The pull of the third dimension is seductive, but awareness will keep you aligned."

"Is that why you're here on Earth, Matria, to help others go to the twelfth dimension?"

"We are all here in service, Kuriozi. How fast or how far any one wants to go, is not for us to decide. But yes. I—*we*—are here to help."

"*We?*" Milan interjected. "Are there more beings like you and Kuriozi here on Earth, helping us?"

"Oh yes. Despite your fear of outsiders, there are many beings on Earth in service to it. Some with form and some without, some as teachers and some as helpers, all here to assist when and if you decide to end your individual and collective suffering. As I mentioned before, no being, even a *Darling*, is allowed to compromise your choice, but once you decide and invite one in, it can help you fulfill it."

"What about dark beings?" Kuriozi asked. "Do they exist, and do we have to invite them in as well?"

"The possibilities of experience and beings are endless," Matria replied. "The question is what do you decide to pay your precious attention to, and what experiences do you want to create for yourself as a result. How much any being matters to you depends on how much you materialize them in your awareness. I personally spend my attention on beings of light and love who I can grow with, learn from, and/or assist."

As she said this, Matria once again put her arms around Kuriozi and Milan, and slowly started to move in joy. Kuriozi followed, and before he knew it, Milan found himself moving his body freely as well. They danced and moved as if they were flowing as one, three seekers—a child, a father, and an elder with consciousness of many lives…

Milan felt like he was in a dream. "I am dancing like I have never danced before," he said, looking into Kuriozi's eyes. "And what's baffling is that there isn't any music playing."

"Yes there is, Dad! We're all dancing to the music of inner connection and love…"

"*Dad!* I am a father to an *Ourian*, the planet I once wanted to conquer…"

"That's right, Milan. Imagine a world where all Little-Everythings are dancing in their own unique way to the music of unity and love, while benefitting from the joyful energy created by the collective dance!"

"You were right Matria, my connection to my multi-dimensionality is what I needed in order to receive the gift of multi-planetary connection, a very close connection as it turns out."

Not much more was said or heard, though a lot was realized. Milan and Kuriozi left Matria's home arm-in-arm, laughing. Even though he had not completed his project—or even decided entirely what it would be—Milan felt complete and fulfilled.

He still had a choice to make—should he take Earthlings to Ours, or transform Earth into the elevated vision of that faraway planet? Milan needed time to fathom his connection with Matria, to say nothing of Kuriozi, and decide. But one thing was certain—he was sitting on top of the triangle of choice, and he saw his options more clearly and deeply than ever before.

YEKI-NABOOD,

YEKI-BOOD

A lot changed in the three years after Milan first met Matria, both in the visible and invisible worlds.

For one thing, the non-human intelligence created by Earthlings and initially called AI, expanded its influence exponentially, far beyond any other technological breakthrough or advance in the history of the planet. But despite its astonishing scope and speed, this inorganic intelligence was still unable to create, relate, or discern at the deepest levels.

For Survivalists, AI amplified fear and panic, deepening their dread in both the visible and invisible realms. For Attentionists, the new intelligence democratized expertise, access, and information, and simplified everyday life in the visible world, while allowing more and deeper connection to the invisible one.

That's because Milan and many of his Attentionist friends were deeply involved in shaping the future of the new technologies, and, with imagination grounded in love, they created a synergetic union of hi-tech and deep wisdom that came to be known as "Wisdomology"—Wisdom + Technology.

Meanwhile, Attentionism spread with extraordinary speed, and Matria, Suksesso, Menso, Lamenti, Devota, Milan, Kuriozi, and many Darlings and other beings poured their energy and resources into helping it expand. Seemingly overnight there were Observations Decks, Neutral-Rooms and Attentionist schools in most communities around the world. The impact on global life and culture was transformative.

One major shift was the decline of MMD—More and More Disease—the greed-fueled mindset that had plagued humanity for centuries. Simplicity and connection to nature replaced the relentless pursuit of excess.

One by one, countries stopped using GDP (Gross Domestic

Product) as their sole measure of growth. Instead, they adopted GDA (Gross Domestic Attention) to gauge progress and well-being.

A variety of AQ or Attentionist Quotient tests became the most widely used and effective indicator of an individual's freedom from fear, access to choice, and quality of life.

Attentionists worldwide regularly practiced choice-authority, breaking free from emotional habits and elevating collective choice-consciousness. With growing skill, they tapped into universal feelings of connection, compassion, and joy.

They also bridged the gap between heart and mind, that age-old split that had bedeviled humans in so many ways. As the Attentionist population approached critical mass, the Heart-Mind of the planet shifted perceptibly, integrating itself and creating and shaping the future with a natural sense of balance, clarity and ease.

In the spiritual realm, truth-seeking became widespread. Many old religious wounds—rooted in segregation and politics—began to heal. Earthlings were overjoyed to discover the common truths shared across faiths and horrified to realize how much pseudo-truth had infiltrated their beliefs.

As more Somethings became Little-Everythings-in-the-making, memories of the Land-of-Unity surfaced, rekindling hopes of returning to the common unity that had always been present. The crisis that once set Milan on his interplanetary mission faded. Butterflies returned, red lightning and drones disappeared, and the pandemic of horrid laughter was replaced by the natural sounds of joy and play.

Milan and his teachers/friends/helpers had much to feel wonderful about, as all of them had done a great deal to bring about the changes described above.

Sukseso passionately mentored Attentionists away from accumulation and toward the true wealth of abundance.

Lamenti and Menso role-modeled the coming together of heart & mind, feminine & masculine, demonstrating how polarity can become unity and serve and benefit all.

Devota devoted most of their energy to holding space for truth seekers of all backgrounds, and teaching peaceful endings of all kinds, including acceptance and celebration of the end of any given round of life.

Kuriozi, young as she was, created play-schools to facilitate the unlearning of Something-ness for adults, and the continuance of fun and play of Little-Everything-ness in children of all ages. She also created an exchange student program between Earth & Ours, allowing youngsters to experience other worlds and homes.

While Milan no longer saw Earth as a doomed planet, he did not give up his idea of going to planet Ours, especially now that he knew it was more evolved than Earth. There, on Ours, with Matria making the introductions, he met Ourians, beings who had physicality and were also looking for ways to de-densify and end their suffering, though on a higher plane.

Milan's experience as an Attentionist, combined with his passion for new frontiers, allowed him to become a suitable inter-galactic Ambassador of Choice, with branches on planet Earth & Ours and plans for expansion to other worlds.

Our group of Attentionists loved traveling as a team to communities on both planets to facilitate the collective transformation from fear to choice. As such, Wisdomology expanded its reach and included the wisdom of different cultures on Earth and Ours. Even though Earth was still emerging from Survivalism, it had much to offer, and Earth and Ours became a model for what could be achieved at a cosmic level through co-intention, co-attention, and co-creation.

Upon returning from their most recent inter-planetary journey, Matria invited the many Attentionists she had mentored to her home. After serving everyone a delicious and nutritious meal from her garden, she told them she was ready to put her body to rest and bring her current physical experience to an end. As a conscious being she knew her time had come.

Matria shared her hopes and plans for her next experience, and reflected on how a new and improved round of physicality—who knew what she would come back as next—a spring, a Darling, a butterfly?—would allow her to better serve the ever-evolving transformational needs of physical beings. She thanked everyone, answered questions, and celebrated her life experiences with them. Then with a wide smile and a clear excitement, she left her body.

All worlds and all beings were touched by the news of the exquisite movement toward unity and Little-Everything-ness that was taking place on Earth, Ours and beyond. Attentionist way-seekers on both planets became way-showers by their mere being and co-creation.

Their journey from Survivalism to Attentionism, separation to oneness, habit to choice, one-dimensionality to multi-dimensionality and inter-galactic sharing, elevated life in all realms of existence, and finally turned our story of *yeki-bood, yeki-nabood* to *yeki-nabood, yeki-bood*....

Instead of matter and density dominating energy, energy and light were guiding matter. The *Invisible* World was leading the way to wellbeing at last.

Never the End!

Abundance vs. Accumulation Being content with what you have while trusting more is available, vs. living in discontent and fear that there will never be enough.

AQ (Attention Quotient) A measure of one's intentional attention: the ability to direct and sustain focus by conscious choice.

Attentionist A person who treats attention as life's greatest power and trains it to rise above fear and reactivity. One who sees facts clearly, uncovers wider choices, and acts on the best path available. The opposite of a Survivalist.

Bellhop Emotions personified: the "bellhop" delivers signals showing how near or far we are from our desired feelings.

Blueprint The guide to creation for Little-Everythings, rooted in love, joy, and unity.

Choice-Consciousness and **Choice-Authority** Knowing we have choices beyond fear, and claiming the authority to act on that knowing.

Cosmic Bank of Wisdom A symbolic storehouse where humanity's wisdom is deposited, preserved, and available to the Whole-Mind.

Darlings Energetic beings who assist Somethings when they choose to reconnect with their Little-Everythingness and move from fear to love.

Eternalist A person who has moved beyond Survivalism and Attentionism, living consciously connected to Source, the Prime Creator, God.

Everything and **Big-Everything** The Source before unfolding Itself & The Source after unfolding into Little-Everythings and Darlings…

Fall-of-Consciousness When the density of fear overpowers the lightness of love.

Genetics, History, and Choice The three aspects of self: the genes we inherit, the experiences we undergo, and the choices we make depending on our consciousness. (See also: Triangle of Self.)

Intention, Attention, Action Three acts of will and choice that need to be aligned in order to create with clarity, coherence, and sustainability.

Land-of-Unity and **Land-of-Separation** Land of Unity is the symbolic home of Little-Everythings before they separated to become Somethings & Land of Separation is Earth, the realm of Somethings living apart from unity.

Little-Everything Human beings creating under the light of Source.

More and More Disease (MMD) A scarcity-driven compulsion to accumulate things without integration or satisfaction. It masquerades as ambition, but "enough" never arrives and the cycle is unsustainable.

Neutral-Room A symbolic space in the mind where an Attentionist calmly and wisely listens to the messages carried by their emotions.

Observation-Deck A symbolic space in the mind where an Attentionist steps back to see the bigger picture and recognize choices beyond fear.

Somethings Little-Everythings who chose not to follow love, unity, and joy, creating instead under separation's limited light or lack thereof.

Source Prime Creator, God.

Spirit The essence of Source.

The "Story" This book's account of who we are and where we come from.

Soul The tiny spark of Spirit present in each human being.

Survivalist A person who lives in survival mode and with self-imposed fear.

Topping-Game The unhealthy urge to "know more" and correct others, driven by accumulation without benefit, integration, or joy.

Transactional vs. Unconditional Relationship with **Source** Relating by exchange (prayer or good deeds to get what we want), vs. relating for its own sake, for the joy of connection.

Triangle-of-Self The interplay of Genetics, History, and Choice.

Truth vs. Reality Truth is the whole of what is, while reality is our partial or distorted version of it.

Whole-Mind and **Rational-Mind** The Whole Mind is connected to the Cosmic Bank of Wisdom, inspiration, intuition, imagination. It is wired for thrival and includes rationality but it is not limited by it. The Rational-Mind is limited, survival-focused, and often fear-driven.

Yeki-bood, Yeki-nabood The visible, material world, and the invisible world of energy.